Beautiful & Hero:

The Infringed Heart

Chimia Y. Hill-Burton

Acknowledgements

All my life ever since I was a child, I have loved to write. From poems, figurative writings, short stories to novels. My passion for writing flourished over the years. I felt my words could speak to the souls and hearts of the world. Through my stories I would express the love, pain, struggle, courage and spirit of the human heart. This novel is humbly dedicated to all the special people in my life, who have always inspired, encouraged and illuminated my creative talent and passion to the art of writing.

Love Always,

Chimia Y. Hill-Burton

Table of Contents

CHAPTER ONE

STARTING OUR HAPPILY EVER AFTER

Nothing in this world would have prepared me for the roller coaster ride I have had in the last two years. He is sound asleep as I lie on his chest. I almost think I am dreaming, looking up at his smooth face. He has to the prettiest eye lashes, his grip around my body tightens as he leans down and kisses my forehead instinctively. A smile comes across my face-- that's my Hero. We have been through so much to be here. Derius's mom Alexandra not liking me. Our separation by order of the court, Derius having to deal with not being with Ayia and me. Sounds of laughter echo down the hallway. I can feel my body being squeezed as Derius wakes up. "Good Morning Beautiful."

All I can do is smile up at him as his kisses my nose. We both stare at each other for a moment. I lean up to greet my Hero with a kiss, when I suddenly feel sick. The look on his face is priceless as he grabs the nearby trash can by our bed. I throw face in it and relieve myself. Derius laughs as he holds my hair back with one hand and rubs my back with the other. "He is giving you one hell of a time huh Beautiful?" I roll my eyes but can't answer as I throw up again. "Urgh I hate having morning sickness." Derius kisses my head and strokes my hair as he takes the trash can from me. "You sit here awhile, I'm going to get you some water." I nod as I watch him hop out of bed, and head to the kitchen.

I lie back down thinking to myself: *We are having another baby, I do hope it is a boy this time.* I still can hear laughter as I finally decide to get up and see my little angel. I get up and head out into the hallway, when Derius meets me. "Beautiful, I said I was bringing you water. What are you doing out of bed?" I smile at him sweetly. "I have to get Ayia breakfast and I still have work today Hero." He shakes his head, then smirks at me. "But I haven't had my breakfast yet." I raise an eyebrow. I know he doesn't think I am in the mood to get busy after throwing up a lung. "Hero, really, do you think I am in the mood for that this morning?" Derius moves closer to me backing me to the wall. I look up at him pleading with my eyes for him not start. Derius grabs me close to him, raises my chin up to him. Rubs my bottom lip with his finger, and leans down. I close my eyes awaiting his kiss.

Derius leans forward, I can sense his presence as he reaches my ear. He blows softly on it then he states "Fine, I'm running late anyway." My eyes fly open as well as my mouth. *No, this punk didn't.* I think to myself as I look up at him. His smile confirms my last thought. Derius kisses my cheek quickly as he runs into the bathroom. Today Derius is going to orientation for Madison College. *I can't believe it's already November. It just seems like yesterday that we were on our honeymoon in Hawaii. Now we are rushing to get ready for work and college. I still have to get showered and dressed for work.* I walk into the living room; my mom is playing with Ayia on the floor and Ayia is rolling around laughing. My mom looks up at me shaking her head. “Girl, what are you doing? You have to get ready for work child.”

I look at myself, I am not even in the mood to get ready for work, but if I want to buy this house Derius and I have talked about I’d better. Soon I see Derius walking into the living room dressed and ready to go. “Okay Beautiful, Princess and Mom. Your Hero, Daddy and Wonderful Son in Law has to go. Love you all.” We all laugh as he kisses each of us goodbye and leaves. I finally get my mind together as I head off to get showered. Soon I am dressed ready for work, I grab my things, kiss my two favorite ladies, and head for the car. I drive off to work, and as I stop at a light; I look over my schedule for the day. Ever since I have gotten promoted to a loan officer. I am really busy; but, soon I can see me being a branch manager.

***

I finally made it into work, when my boss calls me into his office. “Yes, Mr. Totten?” My branch manager smiles happily at me. “Yes Karla, please have a seat. As you know I am looking to appoint a new branch manager here the year after I retire. I have three people in the running for the position. That would be You, Thomas Riley and Patti Smith. I just wanted you to know that you have the best marks with customers here, at Robertson Bank." Smiling thinking to myself *If you think so highly of me, why not give a raise. Come on man I have other things to do besides you fill me with empty hopes.* I continue to listen to Mr. Totten when he says. "However, I have found another position for you that I think would be a better fit for your skills."

I am in shock. As I look at Mr. Totten's face. "You are not replacing me here at the bank are you Mr. Totten?" Mr. Totten looks at me with a smile and nods. "Karla… I interrupt him quickly. "Come on Dexter, I have done excellent work for you these past two years. Haven't I?" Mr. Totten smiles, nodding at me "YES KARLA! That is why I am transferring you to my friend's bank. He needs a branch manager there. You were the first name I thought of when he said that to yesterday when we had lunch together." I could not believe my ears! *Was he serious, was he offering me a branch manager position?!* I couldn't talk let alone breathe for a moment. "ARE YOU SERIOUS?! YOU ARE REFERRING ME

FOR A BRANCH MANAGER POSITION, TODAY !?!" I screamed out loud.

Mr. Totten asked me to lower my voice. "Karla, we are still at work. Calm down, I know you are very excited. My friend wants to meet you today for lunch. Will that be okay with you?" I jumped, grabbing his hand and shaking it, almost jumping up and down. "Of course, I would love to meet with your friend; today is perfect!" Mr. Totten smiled happily "Great so we will go to lunch together today. I will call my friend and let him know and then I will email you with the time." As I was about to say something. Starla from the counter came in the office. "Excuse me. Karla your ten-forty-five is here to see you." I looked over at the clock on Mr. Totten's desk, *yup my client was here*. "Karla, go ahead, take care of business and I will call my friend and email you what time we are going to lunch."

I nodded and headed back to my office. I helped my client with a mortgage loan he wanted to get and as soon as he left. I shut my office door, and blinds and jumped up and down. As soon as I finished it I regretted it dearly. I had to run to the restroom in a hurry. "Okay little boy, Mommy is sorry for making you upset." When I returned to my desk there was an email for me from Totten. We were meeting at a nearby Italian restaurant in an hour. *Yes, I should call Derius and tell him right now, but I think I will wait till after the meeting once it's official.* I calm myself down, I try to continue to do some form of work but I can't. I am too excited about the lunch meeting with my new boss. I wonder what type of person they, I am hoping someone is understanding of my schedule, but then again once I am a branch manager I can leave when I need to as long as my assistant is there. *Man, I cannot believe this.* Time passes by slowly and soon it was time for the lunch meeting.

Mr. Totten knocked on my door. "Okay, Karla, I will see you there, I have to run a quick errand and I will meet you there, okay?" I nodded as I collected my things. "Do you want me to get us a table, since I am on my way there now?" Mr. Totten snapped his finger in approval. "Yes, please get us a table; my friend will probably be there before us, but in the event he isn't; yes, get us a table." I walked out with Mr. Totten and headed for my car. I drove over to the place and asked the host if anyone was looking for Mr. Totten, since I had completely forgot to ask what his friend's name was. They informed me that our party had not arrived yet but would seat me now. So, I sat down and ordered some water with lemon and waited. I checked my makeup and hair. Soon I saw Mr. Totten walk in, he looked around then spotted me as I waved him over. "Sorry Karla, I had to get my son's birthday present before I forget about it." "Oh really Mr. Totten, how old is your son going to be?" Mr. Totten smiles as he pulled out his phone to show off his ten-year-old son Andy. We were chatting away making small walk when I looked away a minute. "DARYL! We are over here." Mr. Totten's friend has just arrived.

I stood up to meet him with a hand shake, and as I stood up and met his eyes I glared at him. Mr. Totten didn't notice as he started to introduce us, his phone rang. "Oh, I'm so sorry Daryl, it's the wife calling me, please give me a few minutes." With that Mr. Totten walked off. Mr. Totten's friend gave me a charming smile. "Well, if it not Karla Na'Shell Jac ..." I interrupted immediately "PHILLIPS!" He was taken back. "Aww that's right you are married now." Daryl rubs his smooth chocolate chin. *My god why did it have to be him, of all people in this world. It had to be Daryl Francis Dewight.* "Yes Daryl, I am married now." Daryl sucks his teeth as he stares at me. "Yeah that's right. But from what I hear he is a mere child." I laugh, folding my arms in front of me. "My HUSBAND is more of a man than you ever claimed to be."

Daryl laughs a little to himself. *GOD help me, he is still so fine.* His dark blue suit fit him so well. I can't help but notice his frame is still the same. Daryl is everything most men desired to be. He is intelligent, business savvy, and charming as hell. "Karla what in the hell are you thinking about?!" *Daryl Dewight was also a narcissistic asshole! He loved his status and himself more than anything or anyone.* I knew better than anyone. Daryl was my fiancé at one time, and he claimed I was the only woman who mattered to him. "YEAH RIGHT! I was the only fool who would put up with his arrogant ass! I thought I was the ONE. Girl, BOO! I was the ONLY ONE he came back to is all. All because of a stupid ring he placed on my finger. I endured his bullshit for six years.

The more I thought about it, the angrier I became about seeing him in front of me now. “So, Daryl, how do you know Dexter?” Daryl finally sitting down, smiles sweetly at me. *Keep it together Karla, he is your new boss.* I half smile back as I await his answer. “Well Dexter and I go back. I have known him since high school. Remember the guy I said was like a brother to me but his mom is white. That’s him, Dexter Totten.” I nodded, “Yeah I remember a lot of things you told me about!” *Karla! Stop it now, you are a happily married woman, you cannot let some dusty blast from the past come in and ruin your day. Smile... BE NICE.* I forced myself to smile at him, believe me it killed me to even look in his direction. Somewhere inside of me I just want to take the fork off the table and stab him several times till I felt better.

“Karla, you are looking so attentively at me? Did you miss me?” *I am so happy I am a chocolate female right now because I know my whole face is red right now. DID I MISS HIM? THIS SON OF BITCH! Come on girl just smile and simply say…*
“Daryl, it’s been a long time since we last spoke or saw each other, but as you can see…” I showed him my beautiful wedding ring. “I am content in the place I have found

for myself over the years." Daryl looked a bit hurt as he cleared his throat and sighed. "YES! Now you know how I felt you BASTARD!" *Lord these hormones are off the chain today. Girl, you said that out loud, look at him he is hurt now. GOOD!* "Karla I am offended. We have a history, and you think that some juvenile could touch what we made together for six years. Come on Karla."

I shook my head, he just did not get it! *Derius is more of man than he could ever dream to be. He is attentive, caring, he is there for me, supports me and above all he loves me. Daryl could not fathom in a million years what that means. Six years, hell he was not even there for six years. I was just holding that title for six years!* "Daryl, I have no idea what you are thinking but for your sake stop it. We are done and over. I am happy now, I have what I need in my life, right now…" Daryl interrupts me, "what you need!?! Please Karla do not make me laugh. What can that boy possible give you that I couldn't or can't?" *I am getting really tired of this asshole calling my husband a boy.* "Daryl, your horns are showing. Derius is not a boy. He is my husband, he is a man. Now, you may not like the fact that I am taken, but you have no choice but to get over it. Besides what do you anyway? I know you are my new boss and all but what exactly do you do for this bank?"

Daryl laughs and then pulls out a business card holder. I watch him pull the business card out then hand it to me. I roll my eyes as he hands it to me. I gasp a little as I read it. *Oh my god! He was not just going to be my boss but sign my paychecks too!* Daryl Dewight owner and CEO of D&D Banking. I could hardly believe what I was reading. *Uh wait scratch that last stupid statement.* Yes, I can, I mean he better had made something of himself after putting everything ahead his life or the people in it! My eyes met his as he smiled at me. "I own D&D Banking. Surprised, are you proud of me?" "Am I proud of him?! Proud, more like disgusted." I attempted to hand back the business card. "Oh no Karla. That's for you."

I took the card and place it in my purse. Before I could say anything, else Mr. Totten came back to the table. "My apologies, Daryl you already know how Beth is about Andy and it's his birthday today. We are trying to get everything situated with his party." Daryl with a laugh, slapped Mr. Totten on the back playfully. It was funny to watch him actually have a tender side. It had been so long since I had seen this side of him. Just then Mr. Totten turns in my direction. "Karla, so what do think? I mean come on I know what you are thinking right? This is an opportunity of lifetime." Daryl looks at me smiling at the comment. "Yes, Karla it is an opportunity of a lifetime. I sure hope you will not waste it." I have to collect myself a minute because I am about to go off. *Waste it huh, this bastard has not changed one bit! He still thinks the sun rises and sets on his narrow ass!* I stand up, looking at both of them. "I'm sorry Mr. Totten, but I do not think I will take the position." Mr. Totten and Daryl are in complete shock. "Karla! You were so excited about getting this position. I mean Daryl is offering a great salary for it. Right Daryl?" Daryl's eyes seem to burn into me as he stares up at me. "Right. I am offering a great salary Karla. Its eighty thousand a year, with perks and bonus. How does that sound?" I fold my arms over my chest and shake my head. "I'm sorry Mr. Totten but I just lost appetite." Mr. Totten looks at me with concern. "Karla, come on now you have to eat."

Daryl chimes in quickly as well. "Yes, please it's the least I can do." I do not want to stand here another minute looking at the smug look on his face. "No thank you…" Mr. Totten interrupts me, "Karla, this is silly, have something eat with us before you go, and let's discuss this." My eyes look at Daryl, as his eyes plead for me to stay and then motions me to sit back down. I sit down for the sake of my boss not that asshole. "Now Karla, talk to us, will you? Why do you not want the position?" Before I can say anything, Daryl states: "I'm sorry if I made a bad impression Karla. I really would like it very much if you would run my Atlanta Branch." Mr. Totten nods at me to take the offer. *I am not sure about all of this, I do not want that asshole to be my boss.* Mr. Totten senses the tension in the room as he states. "Okay, let not talk about it for a moment. Daryl it seems to me that you know Karla?" Daryl stares at me a minute before nodding yes. "Oh yes we went to Whitmore together in Florida before I moved to back to New York, back then I knew her as Karla Jacobs." Mr. Totten laughs then snaps his fingers, "Oh of course, when I first mentioned Karla to you, she was not married yet. Karla, I believe you were pregnant with your daughter at that time right Karla?"

Daryl's eyes darts in my direction as I smile kindly. "Yes, Mr. Totten that is correct. I was pregnant with my daughter Ayia at that time." Daryl face seemed to tighten as he found out I had a child. Mr. Totten nods then looks at Daryl. "Daryl are you okay?" Daryl composes himself quickly as he nods, "Karla how long have you been married?" *You would want to know wouldn't you, fine I will break your heart.* "Not long; I was married the end of October, I am just getting back from my honeymoon really." I watch in delight at the sight, of Daryl's face muscle cringe. He is so pissed off. Then if that was not enough to make him pop Mr. Totten places the candle on the cake for me. "That's right Karla, and how is your pregnancy coming along?" Daryl jumps out of his seat. We both are looking at him, but his eyes never leave my smiling face. Daryl realizes what he is doing, laughs as he states, "Excuse me a moment I have to go to the restroom."

No sooner has he left the table then Mother Nature calls me too. I excuse myself to the restroom. *This child is trying to be the death of me, isn't he?* I try to take a few extra minutes so I will not run into Daryl in the hallway. *POW! Karla you did it, you crushed that smug look right off his face! That is exactly what he gets for trying me like that. I do not need his bullshit job!* I stare in the mirror and collect myself before leaving the restroom. As I walk out, I am startled by Daryl leaning against the door waiting for me. "Are you done bashing me in the restroom Karla?" I am a little surprised at what he just said. "Was he listening to me in the restroom?!" I shake my head and attempt to walk past him, when he pins me to wall, "DARYL!" Daryl covers my mouth with his hand. After looking around making sure it's clear, he removes his hand.

"Karla, stop causing a scene. We are in a fancy restaurant. Now why won't you take my offer to work for me?" I laugh at him when I get a look at the look he is giving me. "Daryl, I am just not sure about working for you with the history we had together." I attempt again to leave but he blocks my way with both hands pressed on both side of me. "Don't run away from me Karla. I mean you marry a child and get knocked up not once but twice. You should have some accomplishments in your life besides being known for robbing the cradle. I am offering you a solid deal here, I know this is what you always wanted." I stare at him and I can't see the boy I knew. He is shallow and pathetic to me now. "Daryl stop calling my husband a child, and for your information I have been doing just fine without your offer. Thank you. Now, will you please move out of my way?"

Daryl takes one deep breath and then moves out of my way. I start to walk away when I feel something; I look back at Daryl who has my arm in his hand. "At least let me feed you, don't just go like that." I know he is not going to let me go if I don't. *Where in the hell was this man when I wanted him, huh?*—is all I can think of as I nod that I will stay. Daryl holds my hand a little longer, before he releases me he rubs my thumb a few times. I take my hand back and head back to the table. Mr. Totten looks concernedly at me. "Karla, Are you okay? Do we need to leave? Is the baby okay?" I calmed his nerves about me going into premature labor. Daryl came back to the table a minute later. "Okay, now Daryl is back we can continue this conversation. Karla, would you please reconsider Daryl's offer? Better yet, what is the matter with offer?"

Daryl looks at me nodding slowly, "Is it the money? If it's the money I can always offer you more. Let's say ninety thousand instead." Here he goes again. *Money is not everything, but I would never expect Daryl to understand that.* "It's not the money; I would have to talk it over with my husband first, is all." *Now that is who I am worried about.* I never really spoke about Daryl the whole time Derius and I were dating. I just have no idea how my Hero is going to react to this. I mean I have an idea how he will react. He will probably be like, "YAY!! Beautiful!" Yeah that is how my Hero would react to me getting this job. "I think I am full, I am going to leave you two for now…" Daryl interrupts me again, "Okay, my final offer one-hundred thousand dollars and I'll throw in a sixty-thousand-dollar sign on bonus. What do you say, Karla?" I am trying to collect my thoughts, *was he serious a hundred-thousand-dollar position with a sixty-thousand-dollar sign on bonus! That was enough money to buy our house in full, with money to spare! Karla, I asked myself, what are you going to do?"*

I keep thinking for a minute as I am about to answer. Daryl throws in one last thing, "take the sign on bonus as a belated wedding present from me. Will you please?" I look at Daryl as I pick up my things to finally leave, "thank you again Mr. Dewight, I will discuss this with my husband and get back to you about your offer." Daryl stands up, walking around to me, then hugs me. As he does he whispers in my ear, "I'm sorry if I made you uncomfortable before Karla, but I really want to see you shine. Please call me with your answer tomorrow." As I breaks his embrace, Daryl smiles at me, "It was good seeing you again Karla. I hope you do consider my offer. I will be waiting for your call." Daryl moves out of my way and I say goodbye to everyone. I look back at Daryl on last time and his slick smug look resurfaces on his face again.

Who in the hell does he think he is Donald Trump!?! I finally escape that nightmare. As soon as I am in the car, I call Angela Green. She is my best friend and she will help me get back to my damn sanity. I listen as the phone rings a few times. "Hello Karla girl, I miss you. How are you?" I laugh that she misses me and then I go in, "Angela, girl you will never believe what happened today?" I wait for Angela to answer me. "Girl, what happened? Is the baby okay? Did someone do something to you, you tell me girl. Because you know me, I will get on a plane and come up there." Okay now I have wait for her to calm down a minute. "No, girl no one did anything, the baby and I are fine, and no plane ride up here for now." Angela clears her throat and then calmly speaks. "So, what is the matter, you sound stressed?"

I can't even hold it in anymore, I have to tell her. "I saw Daryl today." The gasp from the phone is of shock and annoyance. "WHAT DARYL!?! YOU MEAN, 'I DO NOT HAVE TIME FOR ANYONE IN MY LIFE, BUT I JUST WANT YOU THERE UNTIL I DO' DARYL!?!" Angela hit the nail on the head. "Yes girl, and I got one better, I was offered a branch manager position today!" I have to move the phone from my ear, as Angela screams into it. "GIRL NOW THAT IS REAL NEWS! CONGRATS BESTIE!!" I wish I could be as happy, I mean I was when I first heard that I was getting it, now I am not so sure. "Angie! I wish I could be as happy as you are right now. I really do." Angela smacks her lips one time. "Karla Na'Shell Phillips, this is only all you have ever wanted since you took up banking. What is the problem with the job? Not enough money? The location sucks doesn't it?" "Girl if only that were the least of my problems, I think I could handle that. Well, as long as the salary was more than what I make now! Girl, the problem is Daryl, not only is that asshole going to be my boss, but he will also the person who signs my paychecks! Daryl is the CEO D&D Banking!"

Angela's screams could have shattered my windshield that is how loud she was. "WHAT! DARYL IS THE CEO OF D&D BANKING?! Well if we think about it, it could have happened. He damn sure should done something like that. Since the only one he ever talked about when we were in school was how much homework he had to do and not paying any attention to the people in his life!" Angela knew better than anyone about the void that man had left in my heart, with all his promises and lies. "Yeah, girl, I just do not think working for him would be a good idea. I mean the money is amazing and all, but I just do not know." Angela tells me to hold as she quickly take another call. I am headed home now, today was too much anyway. I look at my schedule a minute. *There was nothing else to do anyway.* Soon I hear Angela come back to the phone.

"Okay girl, I'm sorry about that. Now, what would be the big deal in taking the position? I mean do you have see him every day?" I thought about it a minute, no I would not have to see him every day. "No, I do not think so. Last time I checked their main branch was in New York." Angela then asked me about the salary. "Well, he offered me one hundred thousand dollars a year with a sign on bonus." I heard Angela choke as I scream into the phone. "ANGIE! ANGIE! ARE YOU OKAY GIRL!" I hear Angela take a sip of water then come back to the phone. "KARLA! You are going to turn down a hundred-thousand-dollar salary! No, I know you are not doing that girl! What is the real reason that do not want to take this job?"

I knew Angela would know why I was scared to just take it, but I was waiting on her to just say it. "DERIUS!" She screams out loud. "Yes girl, Derius. I just do not know what he is going to say to me working with my ex is all."

Angela sucks her teeth hard. "Karla, do you really believe that Derius is going to tell you no to a job like that with a sign on bonus that could buy you guys a house! Hell no, I know Derius now and I also know that he would stand by you in this. Girl do not worry about Daryl okay, you have Derius right?" A smile curves across my face, as I feel myself glow and laugh. "See girl, I am more than two thousand miles away and I know you are glowing at just the thought of him. You have a man in your life now that makes time for you, loves you unconditionally and supports you whenever you need it. However, hello, if Daryl offered me a position I would take it."

Then an idea came to my mind. "ANGIE! What if I got you a position with me?! I need an assistant and then you could move here." Angela laughs on the phone at my suggestion, "Girl, if Daryl pays me eighty thousand dollars, I will take you up on your offer. If he pays me more, I am already packed." Angela laughs out loud as I pull up in front of the apartment. "Well Angie, I will talk it over with Derius tonight and see how he feels about it, then I will make a decision." I listen as my friend tells me she loves, me and talk to me soon then hangs up the phone. I sigh deeply as I collect my things to go in the house. No sooner as I open the door, a little someone is there to greet me. "MOMMY!" Ayia yells as she run into my arms. I kneel, picking her up, and giving her a kiss. "Karla Na'Shell Jacobs Phillips, put that girl down, you are pregnant remember." I do as my mom says, then stretch and sigh as I look at her. "Karla, what is the matter Honey?" I do not want to bother my mom with my long annoying day.

"Nothing Momma, I am just hungry, I didn't eat much at lunch today." I walk past her and head for the kitchen to fix me something to snack on. Once I am in the kitchen I am looking inside of the fridge, I can hear my mom talking to Ayia. "Now Honey, you sit here and watch TV while I go in here and talk to your Momma okay." I hear Ayia laugh sweetly saying, "Yes Ma'am." Soon my mom meets me in the kitchen. I am snacking on yogurt. "Okay now Karla, spill it child. What is bothering you?" I knew better than anyone, you cannot hide anything from Ellie Mae Jacobs. "Okay Momma, I was offered a Branch Manager position today." My mom's eyes were as big as silver dollars. "Karla that is amazing news! Why do you look so unhappy about it child?" I continued to eat my yogurt, as I explained about whom I would be working for. "Momma, the position is not the problem, nor is the money." My mom looked confused as she asked. "Well how much are they offering you?" Sitting the empty yogurt cup down. I looked at the ground and then at my mom. "A hundred thousand dollar a year with a sixty-thousand-dollar sign on bonus."

Mom screams so loud that she scares Ayia. "Oh my god! Ayia, honey it's okay grandma was just a little excited okay." I hear Ayia say okay then she goes back to watching her T.V. "Momma! Not so loud." My mom agrees but looks at me like a crazy. "Karla, they offered you that much money and you are scared to take it! Child with that kind of money you and Derius can buy that house you want on the bonus alone!" I am thinking the same thing as my mom explains it to me. But I have not told her the real reason I do not want the job yet. "Momma the real reason I do not want this job is because Daryl Dewight will be my boss." The smile that was one my mom's face disappeared quickly at the mentioning of that name. "Karla, you mean to tell that no good fool, who placed that gold ring on your finger as placeholder that he was never going to collect is your BOSS honey!"

When my mom put it that way, it sounded more and more like a bad idea. "Not just that Momma, Daryl is the CEO of the bank I am going to work for." Now my mom's expression is complete surprise and irritation. "You mean to tell that arrogant punk is not just your boss but the man who will sign your paychecks! Oh, Karla I see why you don't want that position at all." I am so happy that my mom agrees with me. "Yes Momma, Daryl is the CEO of D&D Banking." That statement made my mom throw her hands up in the air. "Not the bank I am now banking at?! That D&D Bank, is owned by Daryl?!" This news is not going well at all for my mom. Then again it was not going well for me either. I began to have second thoughts about working there again. *Even if the money was great and it is. Should I really put myself in that type of environment?* My mom kept shaking her head at the news. "Karla, I am not going to tell you what to do, because you are grown. However, I am going to tell you this, talk to Derius about it first."

"Momma, I am going to talk to him about it. I mean I want the job even though I will be working for Daryl. It's just that I never told Derius about Daryl." I knew that look, my mom is giving at me like I was in real trouble. "Child you have been with this young man all this time, and never told him about Daryl!" Shaking my head, I explained. "Well Momma with everything that went on with Derius, with his mother, being pregnant with Ayia and court. When was there time to talk to him about Daryl?" My mom thought it over a minute, she knew I was telling the truth. Besides, I was so busy being happy and confused that Daryl never even came to mind. "Well Honey, I guess that is true, but now that rat has resurfaced it's time to tell Derius about. Take it from me baby, men do not like their women around their exes, I know. You remember Mr. Samuel, don't you?"

I had to think for a minute but I believe I did. "Oh yes Momma! Dr. Samuel." My mom snaps her fingers, nodding. "That is right, now I worked at the Hallandale Hospital for twenty years. My first and only job out of nursing school was that hospital. On my first day, I saw Samuel. Now by that time, I had been married to your daddy a long time. Well I never told any of you this, but Samuel was my first love before I met your dad. Samuel and I broke up because he cared more about becoming a doctor than being my husband. So, when we met again at the hospital, it was the first day for us both. Samuel was so excited to see me, I was working on his ward. When I got home that night I told Robby J about Samuel. Your daddy was so pissed off."

"Honey, he told me that he did not like it. He told me he was against the whole thing. I told him to stop being foolish and asked if he trusted me. Robby J, your daddy, told me these words: "I trust you Ellie, I do not trust him. No matter what length of time it has been, no matter what the status of a relationship you are in now. When a man wants a woman, he will go after her." So, Honey talk to Derius, because men know men." I had to take those wise words to heart, even though I am sure Daryl has someone else. I have to talk to Derius about this before I can make a decision. I gave my mom a hug and thank her for the advice. Then after checking on Ayia, went into the bedroom and text Derius; "Hero, when you get home, we need to talk."

CHAPTER TWO

CHALLENGING NEW EVENTS

"Okay Beautiful, Princess, and Mom. Your Hero, Daddy, and Wonderful Son in Law has to go. Love you all." I say as I rush out the door, to the car, and head to orientation. Man, I cannot believe I am about to start college this year. Time sure flies by. I head to my new school, Madison University. After what seems like an eternity to get to, I am finally here. I park in the parking lot, get out and check my phone. "Good, I have fifteen minutes before it's time to start. I better call Franco because he is always late." I dial up my best friend and brother Franco Byars. The phone rings for a while and then he answers. "What's up DK?" I roll my eyes thinking to myself "Now, I know this brother did not forget about orientation today." I laugh to myself as I ask. "Franco, where are you?" I listen to Franco yawn loudly, then stretch. In the background, I can hear Shatoya screaming at Franco that they will be late.

"SHIT! DK I AM ON MY WAY, GIVE ME LIKE FIFTEEN MINUTES!" All I hear next is the phone hang up. I exhale, as I take in the campus's view. My mom talked about this place all the time. Even when my dad was still alive, she wanted me to go to Madison University. "Well mom, your son is here. Madison University." I like campus so far, it's wide, green, and the air is different in a way. I can envision success here, I can also envision my hand going upside Franco's big head when he finally gets here too. I take a few minutes to look around for the Martin building where orientation takes place. "Damn this place is so huge, where is it?" The sound of my five-minute alarm rings, I turn it off shaking my head. I can hear a car coming in my direction as I see Franco park. "DK! Man, I am sorry I am late!" We do not have time for that now as I yell. "Come on man; we are already late."

Franco and I run around a minute looking for the Martin building. Soon we realize we are lost. Franco sees someone walking in our direction. "Hey man, let's ask him where it is?" I agree as I call out to the brother walking towards us and see he is on his cell phone. "Hey, excuse me, but do you know where is the Martin building?" The brother nods as he states. "You must be a freshman. I am Robby; I am headed that direction right now. So, follow me." I let out a sigh of relief as we follow Robby to the correct building. He explains to us he is a junior there, and he is our escort around campus today as we reach the building. We are about to walk in when Robby laughs. "Hey, I know you are not about to go in there now, are you? I mean since its orientation, Professor Blair, would let you slide this time. However, if you were late for his class, no way it's an automatic zero. Since it's all about time management, and history of the school, let's just wait out here till the tour starts."

Franco looks at me then shrugs his shoulders. I look at Robby, then state. "So, you are not going in?" Robby shakes his head slowly. "Hell, No! Professor Blair will call me when he is done. We have been through this many times before." No sooner as Robby says that, his cell phone rings. "See, what did I tell you?" As Robby answers the phone and lets Professor Blair know he is outside waiting. I turn to Franco and swiftly smack him upside his head. "Ow DK, what in the hell is that for?!" I point my finger at him, then at my watch. "That was for being late. Come on, man! We discussed this last night; we would come early to get our schedules and be at orientation." Franco raises both hands in defense.

"Yeah, I know man, but Shatoya wasn't feeling good when I got off the phone with you. So, I had to take care of her until she finally went to sleep. Then after that, I finally passed out. I was so tired I slept past my alarm, till you called. Then after getting dressed, in the car and all Shatoya gets in with me". I am like, "where are you going?" She rolls her eyes and tells me I have to drop her off at HER orientation! Now you already know Shatoya is going to Stephenson. So, I had to drop her off first then come here to meet you." I snap my fingers at that the part. I had forgotten Shatoya was attending Stephenson. "Okay Franco, you good. I forgot about Shatoya starting school too." With that, I dropped it, as the tour went underway. We walked with the group looking at our new school. We found the cafe, the library, the admin offices and our classrooms.

Before we knew it, the tour was over, and everyone headed to get their schedules. After Franco and I got our schedules, Franco reminds me he needs to see his basketball coach. Robby agrees to show us where it is as we are walking I see Dexter. Dexter sees us too and runs over to us. "What's up peoples, Robby, I see you are with these two knuckleheads." Robby points at us laughing. "Dex, you know these two?" Dexter nods as he walks over giving us pound. "Yea, I knew them back in Hallandale before I graduated. Hey, Franco are you headed over to meet the coach?" Franco nods as Dexter says he will take us over there. We all walk together to the gym. As we walk, I ask Robby how he knows Dexter. "Oh, I became roommate this year. I had some financial issues, and Dexter told me to help him with his bills in exchange for a room. I agreed."

Yeah, that sounds like Dexter all right, he would love a roommate to help him with all those bills he runs up. We finally make it to the gym, as soon as I walk in, I feel a sense of peace. I love playing ball, more than anything else. Well, almost anything as Beautiful and my Princess's heads pop into my mind. I look over the squad and can pretty much tell who Junior Varsity is and who is Varsity. We all walk over as Dexter introduces us to the coach. "All right Franco, this is Coach Orlando. Coach, your new player Franco Byars." Coach Orlando looks a lot like Morgan Freeman in "Lean on Me." Coach Orlando shakes Franco's hand, then looks over at me. "You look familiar, what is your name?"

I point at me myself and Coach Orlando nods. "I'm Derius Phillips sir." The Coach thinks a moment though he doesn't look familiar to me at all. He suddenly snaps his fingers at me. "You were the one who had his scholarship first, pointing at Franco." I am kinda embarrassed as I nod slowly. "Yes, sir I did, but circumstances arose and I had to give up my scholarship." Coach Orlando nods then points at me again. "It wasn't a criminal circumstance was it?" Shaking my head quickly, no not that, thanking god. "No, sir! Just something more important came up." I watch as Coach Orlando, nods, then rubs his head. "Byars! I have two openings for Varsity.

I am giving you a shot since you made Varsity your last year of school. Derius!" I turn my head quickly in the coach's direction. "Yes, sir?" He looks me over a while then asks. "Can you still play son?" I smile as I nod quickly that I could still play. Of course, I can still play, basketball was like breathing and I could never forget how to breathe, so I could never forget how to play ball.

Coach Orlando smiles at me then snaps at a guy to come over. Franco shoves me laughing at the guy. "Derius, look it's your twin brother." I look at this guy standing next to the coach. He looked like an older version of me. "Okay, Derius you are going to play a quick game of twenty-one with Philip here, okay." Now, this caught me off guard, as I look down at my casual kicks I had on. "Coach, I can't play in these, I need my sneakers." Franco shoves me again as I stare at him with a frown. "Come DK; you can play in those for today. Stop being like that." The coach and Philip just shrug at me as I agree to play. I snatch off my shirt I was wearing. I lean down, tightening my shoelaces on my shoes thinking to myself. *Okay Derius, remember you are playing in these, don't do too many fancy moves. Well, I guess one or two won't hurt.* The feeling I was getting just being on the court again was great. As I walk up to Philip, I laugh. He frowns at me as he asks; "Man, what is so funny?" I wave my hand at him.

"I am just laughing because we look alike, you said your name is Philip, right?" Philip nods, as he looks me over, he laughs too. I guess he sees the resemblance too. "Well, my last name is Phillips," I state with another laugh as we square up to jump for the ball. Philip laughs again, then smirks. "Well then, don't take this whipping too hard little brother." I do not get to respond as the ball goes in the air, we both jump for it, and I get it. I start down the court as soon as I am at half point. I hear Franco yell out. "FROM THE MIDDLE, DK!" I pause, planting my feet, jump up releasing the ball and watching it sail beautifully into the basket. A roar of cheers erupts from the sidelines as I run to retrieve the ball. Philip has it now, and he is trying to dance around me, talking crazy shit.

I shake my head, nodding as I snatch the ball from him and go up for a layup. We continue the game for a while. Philip is pretty good, he is a challenge, but not much because I am whipping him pretty severely. Soon the game is over, and I won. It feels good to be back on the court. I give Philip a handshake with a shrug and a smile. He nods as he shrugs back saying "Ight little brother, you can ball, I have to give you that." He slaps me on the back and returns to the team waiting to clown him on the sidelines. I turn to see Franco hand high in the air; I slap him a high-five as we walk back over to the coach. "Derius! That was amazing son! Philip is my first-string captain on my Varsity team, and you broke him down!" I laugh, then look down at my shoes. "I could have played better with my sneakers on." Coach Orlando's mouth drops as he looks over at Dexter and Franco pointing at me. "He could have played better!?!" Dexter and Franco nod together as I look over my shoes again to make sure I didn't scuff them up.

I can hear Dexter tell the coach. "Oh yeah coach, Derius plays way better with his sneakers. I am surprised he agreed to play in those. He hates playing in his casual kicks." I look back at everyone staring at me. Coach Orlando walks over me, slapping me on the back. "Son, I have a proposition for you. I am short a man on Varsity. He was killed in a car accident right after he accepted his scholarship. So, if you want the position as second point guard, well kid it's yours." My reaction on my face must have been priceless because everyone was laughing at me. I could not comprehend what had just happened. I blink twice before I respond. "Coach! Coach are you serious?!" Everyone laughs at me again. I shake my head because it is funny. I feel like crying at the chance to play again, but I hold it in.

Coach Orlando laughs a little then says. "I'm serious; you outshined my best player. I need a man like you on the team. This is Philip's last year playing with me, and soon, I will need a new captain. With my spots filled for Varsity, then I can give the other freshman's a better run to improve their skills to step up. What do you say?" The only thing I could say at that moment. "YES, SIR!" After that the coach went back to practice with the team, telling Franco and me we had practice next week starting Monday. We all left the gym once we were outside. I still could not believe it. I was going to play ball again. "Man, I cannot believe what just happened. Someone pinch me." Suddenly out of nowhere, a burning, stinging sensation came from my left arm. Dexter just punched me in the arm. "Ow, Man! I said pinch me not punch me!" He drapes an arm around my neck and squeezes. "Aw come on Derius! At least now you know you are not dreaming right!"

I elbow Dexter in the stomach to get him off me as I look at Franco. "We are going to be playing on the same team this time." Franco high-fives me then hugs me. I hug my brother. Franco sees how much that last statement meant to me. "DK, I know you, I saw how you teared up hearing you are going to play again. I know how you feel." I slap him on the back as he releases me. Dexter and Robby stare at us for a minute in a weird way. Franco and I look at each other for a minute, then laugh out loud. Waving our hands at them stating. "This is a brother thing; you would not understand." They stare at each other, then shrug together. Now Franco and I are now looking at them. Shaking their heads together. "It's a roommate thing you guys wouldn't understand." That makes both of us laugh as we walk by the track. Robby looks then his mouth flies open. "Damn, look at the new fresh meat on Stephenson's cheerleading squad."

I am busy looking at my schedule. "Okay so I have Integrated Math first, then Literature, Intro to Sports Medicine, and Biology. Damn, that is a lot of classes for the first semester, but the times are okay. I will not have to change too much of my schedule at work to fit in basketball. I look up at Franco to ask him when he has a break between classes when I notice he is staring at me already. My eyes cut to Robby and Dexter who are also staring at me. "Why are you all staring at me?" Robby then points over at the field. "Man, she is staring at you hard as hell Derius." I roll my eyes as I look in the field's direction, sure enough, there is this light skin chick staring at me, licking her lips. She is slightly taller than Karla, thicker too, especially in the thighs and ass. She turns around so I can get a better view and what a view it is as she winks at me then drops into a full split.

"DAMN!!" I hear as the guys yell at her. I nod in approval. I mean she is bad and all but I have no interest in that. I turn to get ready to leave when Robby grabs my arm. "Where in the hell are you going!?! Go over there and talk to her, MAN!" I shake my head, pulling away from him. "Nah, I'm good, not interested." Robby grabs me again then drags me back, turns me to the field. "Man, what in the hell do you mean you are not interested?! Man, you are crazy, if you do not go over there and holla at that!" Robby looks closely at the chick again; he snaps looking at Dexter. "Hey Dex, I think I know that girl?" Dexter shrugs as Robby looks closely at her. "OH SHIT! I KNOW THAT GIRL. THAT'S CRAZY ASS TOMMY J'S, DAUGHTER!" Dexter's eyes go wide as he looks back at the girl who is still damn staring at me. I shake my head waiting for someone to explain. Dexter walks over then places a hand on my shoulder. "Derius, do you remember when you and Franco were freshman, and I told you two the story about the guy who killed a teacher and got away with it. You two thought I was lying at the time."

Franco slaps me on the back, and I snap my fingers because I remember that story. "NO!! Dexter that wasn't real! Was it for real?!" Dexter nods then points over at the chick who is STILL looking at me! "That's Tommy J Johnson's daughter." Robby nods then looks at me shaking his head. "That is Johnisha Johnson. Tommy J is a drug lord here in Atlanta and that girl over there is known as the ATL PRINCESS, she gets whatever she wants because she attends Stephenson, her dad supports both schools." Was this for real? These schools would take money from a drug dealer?! "Man, are you serious; they would do that?!" Robby goes into a little more detail. "Look, Madison and Stephenson are the top black schools. They do not want trouble of any kind and because technically they do not know of Tommy J's background, and the donations are always accepted anonymously. Shit man, the gym you walked out of Tommy J help build. The uniforms, we wear, the bus we ride to games in and the catering service that comes, Tommy J help supply. Anything Johnisha is involved in her dad supports hundred percent. I heard a rumor about when Johnisha was in middle school and on the cheer team. Her dad bought them a new gym because Johnisha tripped on a loose plank on the floor in the gym."

Now, this is all I needed, another crazy ass spoiled brat hounding me again. Fuck that; I am going to stay out of this one, THIS damn time! I heard my cell phone; I had a message from Beautiful; "Hero, when you get home, we need to talk." Oh shit, I wonder what that's about? I turn to guys then wave, I gotta go. Everyone agrees, as we walk back toward the parking when I hear someone call out to us. We all turn to see this female running in my direction. "Well, so you are just going to check me out and not say hello." I laugh at myself a little as I shrug. She throws her hair back over her shoulder, with a feisty look in her eyes. "My name is Johnisha, and you are?" She walks up on me closer and I catch a whiff of her perfume. *OH, DAMN THAT SMELLS NICE! GET A GRIP DERIUS! BACK UP A LITTLE!* I step back a few steps from her as I look back at Franco. "Well, Johnisha is it? That is confidential information that is only released on a need to know basis."

Johnisha folds her arms in front of her, smirking, "well, this is a need to know basis, I need to know you." She licks her lips seductively. *OH, HELL NO! SHE IS TRYING ME! GOTTA GET OUT OF HERE NOW.* I smile a little as I bite my lower lip that makes her gasp as little. "Well I am sorry, but I'm not granting access to that information." I walk off with these fools at my heels. Once we are a good distance from her, I rub my head, as Robby asks me. "Man! What is the matter with you!?! I would have tapped that right then and there. MY GOD, she is so fine!" I shake my head at that fool as I state: "Maybe because I have more respect for more important things than ass man." Robby steps in front of me then stares at me a moment. "Nigga! What could possibly be more important than getting some fresh ass man!" I raised my left hand and showed off my wedding ring. "I know my vows man!"

Robby points at my ring; then at me, he looks perplexed as he asks me. "Wait! How old are you, man?" Of all the questions to ask, he asks me that. "I'm eighteen." Franco, Dexter and I watch Robby flip out. "YOU'RE EIGHTEEN, AND YOU ARE MARRIED?! OH MY GOD! WHAT IN THE HELL DERIUS?! YOU JUST GOT TO COLLEGE MAN!" I could see how that could throw people off. So, I really can't get mad at Robby for going off like that. "I fell in love man, I mean yeah, I got to college, but I am married with a little girl and one on that way." Robby threw his hands in the air and just sat on the grass. "Derius! Man, that was just stupid!" Okay now, this nigga was about to get on my nerves. "How was that stupid?! I am in love with my wife; we have a beautiful child together. Please explain how it was stupid." Robby sits on the grass shaking his head, then jumps up looking at me. "YOU WERE THE ONE DEX TOLD ME ABOUT! YOU'RE THE NIGGA WHO MARRIED THE OLDER WOMAN RIGHT?!" My eyes cut in Dexter's direction as he looks away and shrugs. This nigga here! He has told his crazy nigga my business. "Yes, I got married to an older woman, who is my wife." Robby stood up then shook his head at me stating. "Nigga, you are whipped!"

Now I have been called many things while dating Karla but whipped was never one of them. "What?! How am I whipped Robby?! HUH!?! Because I fell in love with a beautiful older woman, I have to be whipped. Oh, it's not possible for me to pull a woman that age?!" Robby gave me a round of applause then stated. "Okay, now, I think about it, it is pretty fucking impressive. I have never dated anyone older than twenty, but to pull a what

twenty-nine-year-old. Yeah, I give that one to you." We all laugh at that compliment as we reach the parking lot. "Franco, now we are playing on the same team this time, you know what we have to do." Franco holds his stomach tightly shaking his head.
"NO DK, Not that! Not SSDs PLEASE!" Robby and Dexter laugh but have to ask. "Okay, what are SSDs?" Franco rolls his eyes as he explains our high school workout. "SSDs are Suicide Session Drills. Derius came up with it when he was trying to get me on Varsity in high school. We have to run the stairs of the football bleachers only until they stop, then across the roll and back up the remaining stairs to the next set. We do that in a diagonal line all the way across. Then push-ups, lunges, squats, and then basketball drills! This nigga DK tried to kill me twice!"

I can't help but laugh at Franco whining about our workout. "Yea, he passed out on me twice but he made Varsity and got my scholarship to go here. So, it was all worth it in the end right Franco." Franco flashes me his classic "Fuck You DK," face and I laugh. Robby nod after hearing about the workout. "Hey, do you mind if I join you? It's could do me good before football starts." We agree as me all side-eye Dexter, who shakes his head. "Hell, Nah! I'm not getting up at four-thirty in the fucking morning to exercise. FUCK THAT!" Everyone starts laughing till I think of something that would get him to do it. "All right Dexter man, I mean if you do not want to then cool, but Angela likes guys who are in shape man." Dexter's head immediately turns to look at me, as I nod at him. "For real Derius, you had to bring her fine ass up, didn't you? FUCK IT! Okay, I will go. The things I do for a woman." I laugh out loud again as I say proudly. "Endurance!"

As I open my car door to finally go home, I turn to them laughing. "Hey, that's probably why I could pull Karla the way I did, endurance!" They all burst out laughing slapping me high fives. "I mean, she had to have something besides my charm that kept her happy right?!" I am done as I get in the car and drive home. As I drive home from the school, I think to myself. "I think you will enjoy college Derius." I pick up my phone and dial-up Beautiful. "Hello, Hero." The sound of her sexy voice, makes me want to be home even faster. "Hey Beautiful, how was your day?" Karla clears her throat, then answers me in a slightly depressed voice. "It was okay, are you on your way home now?" I tell her I will be there in a little while. She tells me she doesn't want to talk about her day till I get home. "What is the matter Beautiful, did something happen at work?!" Karla refuses to talk about it right now. "Let's talk about it when you get home okay, Hero. I am going to lie down, the baby has me feeling sick again. Love you."

Karla hangs up the phone. "What in the hell happened that she doesn't want to talk about it over the phone?" I dislike the tone in her voice. Hmm, okay, Derius, what can this Hero do to save the day this time? I think it over then it hits me as I make a quick stop by the store. I grab a few items and head straight home. I park the car, grab my stuff, and unlock the door. It's past six pm when I finally make it through the door. "Daddy!" is the first thing I hear when I come in. "Aw it's my Princess, yes your daddy missed you." As I kiss Ayia on the cheeks and give her a big hug. "Now where is my Beautiful?" I walk down the hallway and ran into my mother-in-law Mrs. Elle coming out of the bathroom. "Oh well, she is definitely beautiful, she is my mother-in-law." Ms. Elle blushes a little as she hits me, and I give her a kiss on the cheek. "Derius, you are such a sweet boy." Now that is the only woman, besides my mom who can call me a boy and still make me feel special.

I finally reach my bedroom door and knock softly. I can hear my Beautiful moaning unhappily on the other end. I open it slowly, to see Karla lying on her side, pouting at me. I smile as I walk over to the edge of the bed and kneel down to her face. "Hero, you're home. I do not feel good." I softly kiss her forehead, then whisper to her. "I have a surprise for you Beautiful, can you give me a few minutes?" She looks up at me with a curious look then nods she will wait for me. I kiss her nose then get and prepare her surprise in the bathroom. Karla has been complaining about not feeling good for a while. Morning sickness, can be the worst. I clearly remember being sick as a dog when she was pregnant with Ayia. So, I get out the foot spa I just bought for her. I then toss in some lavender bubbling beads in. I walk into the room with the spa and plug it up.

"No peeking Mrs. Phillips, you hear me?" She smiles at being called by my last name. She loves hearing me say that to her, more than Beautiful sometimes. I walk back into the bathroom. I get out the massage oils, nail polish and vibrating hand massager put them on a silver tray as I return to the bedroom. After checking on foot spa, I ask her to sit up for me. Karla looks at me as I place the tray on the bed. "Hero, what are you doing?" I place a finger to my beautiful wife's lips as I silence her. "No talking, just let me relax you for now." She laughs, but does not speak, as I help her put her feet in the foot spa. I can see the tension leave your face as she relaxes. Next, I take the massage oil, massaging her hands. "So Beautiful, you wanted to talk to me about something earlier. What is that you could not talk to me on the phone about?" The smile leaves Karla's face as she tenses up in my grasp. "Do I have to tell you right now? I am trying so hard to just relax right now." I shake my head as I continue with the massage. "No, go on and tell me, I am going to relax you either way Beautiful."

Karla takes a deep breath, then smiles at me. "Uh oh, what are you up to? You only give me that I love Hero, do not get mad at me face, when you have done something." Karla laughs at me, then kisses my forehead. "You know me too well, Hero." I smile at her, kissing her nose slightly as I look into her brown eyes. "Well I am your husband; shouldn't I know you better than anyone else." She takes her hands out of mine and wraps them around my neck. Bringing me close to her, she kisses me. No matter, how many times our lips touch each other. I feel like it's our first time. Karla then leans back from me, stares at me then says. "I was offered a Branch Manager position today." I blink, as I hug her tightly in my arms. "Baby! That is amazing news, why so depressed about it? Is the money not worth the job or something? Don't tell me we have to move? "

Karla shakes her head at me then smiles. "No, we do not have to move, the money is amazing. They offered me a one thousand dollars a year salary plus a sixty-thousand-dollar sign-on bonus." I had to sit down now, wow, my baby had an offer like that! "Beautiful, that is more than I could have imagined them ever offering you." Karla still looked on edge, she didn't look excited about this opportunity. "Okay, it's not the salary, or the location, then what is it? Talk." Karla just stares at me for a minute, like she analyzes my thoughts. "It's the person I will work for. He is my ex-fiancé. His name is Daryl Dewight." Okay, now I could see why she didn't just tell me about it on the phone. "Okay, so he will be your new boss?" Karla nods quietly at me, then takes my hands in hers. "I know I have never mentioned him before but, Hero, I was soo busy being happy, and confused with you he never came to my mind till now."

Kissing her hands, I smile at her. Karla was worried how I would feel about her working with an ex. I am feeling a bit on edge about it, but I am not going to let that stop Karla from taking this promotion. I trust my baby, she can handle this, I know she can. "Okay, so are you going to take the job?" Karla looks at me pleading with her eyes she does want the job. "Are you okay with me taking it, Hero?" I jump up, hugging her tightly, and whispering in her ear. "You better take it, I won't have you blaming me for not letting you achieve your dreams. I am here to support dreams always, Beautiful." Karla hugs me tightly, laughing at me. I know that she wants to take the job. Even though I do not want to see her work with this guy if he has her is on edge. I know my Beautiful is a strong, beautiful, intelligent woman. In some ways, even though she may not know it, she reminds me of my mom. "I am so happy that you are happy for me and this new position. Now we can buy the house of our dreams! That is right with that sign-on bonus we can buy the house outright and have no mortgage!"

Suddenly I remembered the news I had to tell Karla myself. I let her go then took a towel, drying her feet. I dripped massage oil on them as I massage them. She smiles at me as I dry them. I then take the towel and wipe the remaining oil off her feet. Once I finish I take the nail polish and painted them myself. Karla's mouth flies open as she watches me paint her toes. "Do you like it, Beautiful?" She nods at me happily, and now everything is back to normal. "Well Beautiful, I have news for you too, but when I tell you, remember I am painting your toes, okay." Karla nods curiously, then tries to analyze me again. "You know you can't read minds right, Karla Phillips." I tickle her foot a little, she kicks me and I grab her foot. "HEY! I told you not to move, did you mess up my work?" I look over her polished foot. No, it's okay.

"You tickled me, what else could I do, Hero. Now, what is it you have to tell me?" I finish painting her toes, then I massage her legs mainly her calves. "Well, as you already know I went to orientation today with Franco. Franco had to go see his new basketball coach and while I was there, he asked me to play a game with his top player." Karla claps, leans down, kissing my cheek. "I knew you were amazing, Hero." I smirk, as I kiss her, then lean back from her, "Yes, I was amazing even though I played in my casual kicks! Well, I amazed the coach so much, he offered me a spot on the Varsity team! I am going to be a Point Guard! Karla screams loudly, hugs me tightly, planting kisses all over me. "HERO YOU ARE GOING TO PLAY ON THE TEAM!!!!!!! YAY!"

Karla is so loud her mom bust in the room. "What?! What in the hell is the matter child!" Karla shakes her head as she runs over to mom explaining I will be playing college basketball this year. "OH DERIUS! THAT IS GREAT HONEY! COME HERE!" I get up and hug my mother-in-law. Suddenly a little girl comes running in at top speed. I pick her up and kiss her cheek. "Aren't you supposed to be in bed right now, Princess?" Ms. Elle takes Ayia, telling us she will put her back to bed before she leaves. Once they are gone, I jump on the bed and climb on top of Karla. "Hero, what are you doing?" The look in my eyes is telling her just what I want from her. She laughs as she shakes her head.

"Hero, I know you did all of this for me, but I am really not in the mood tonight." I huff a bit to myself then I get an idea. There are two ways to get me off tonight. I smile at Beautiful devilishly as I sink under the covers. She goes to say my name and I place my hand over her mouth. "Don't say a word, Mrs. Phillips." She looks down at me, shaking her head. Whispering for me to stop playing, and that she is serious. The smirk on my face confirms to her that I am not stopping. She is going to have to take it and enjoy it. I know I am, as I disappear under the sheets. Karla keeps fighting me, as she wiggles, twist and even attempts to lock her legs closed from me. I crawl up to her face, placing softly kisses on her neck, ear, and lips. I draw her into my trap. My lips move down, kissing her on her breast, her stomach, the sides. Biting into her skin and hearing her forcibly moan. I am almost to where I want to be when she says with a giggle. "Derius, I am not playing with you don't."

Sorry Baby I am not taking no for an answer, as I take my prize for at least an hour. Once I am satisfied I get up, kiss Beautiful goodnight and try to go to sleep. I wake up an hour or so later with a heavy feeling. I look down at my chest and its Karla lying on me. But I already know that is not the feeling that is starting to bother me. *Karla is going to take that job because I said it was okay, but am I sure about this? I mean I trust Beautiful, I do but I do not know this nigga or if he even is one. She didn't say if he was black or white, and right now, that is not the point. The point is that I have no idea what shit this man has up his sleeve. I know one thing though if he fucks with my baby the wrong way. He is going to have me to deal with. I am not worried, Karla will have this all under control. Won't she?*

CHAPTER THREE

LITTLE THINGS

It has been almost a month since Derius, agreed for me to take the position at D&D Banking. I have adjusted well if I say so myself. I have my own office and Hero sent me a huge bouquet of roses on my first day here. I still have them in my office. I have taken excellent care of them. Well, I am happy for the most part, for one there is no Daryl. *Thank you, there is a God!* He is in New York taking care of another bank's location, but just because he is not here does not mean he doesn't call or email. Daryl calls or emails me every morning. Mostly for reports he needs but also to tell me good morning — that part I can live with because when he calls I usually just stare at my family portrait on the desk of Hero and me with Ayia. My doctors' appointments have been good too; even though I have another one in two months and

I can find out what I am having. I think it's a boy though, because that is what Hero thinks it is.

Speaking of Hero, I have a game to go to tonight. I believe this is the second or third game of the season. I lose count, with all the screaming and my hectic schedule here at work. Once I took the position, I asked if Angela could be my assistant. Daryl agreed, saying: "As long as you are happy Karla." He gave her a great salary with a sign-on bonus. Angela walks in wearing a new outfit. "Karla, girl what do you think of this outfit? It was on sale at Macy's and I had to have it." I shake my head at my best friend as she sits in the chair in front of my desk. "Girl, I would have never dreamed of having such a great job and working with my best friend too." I had to agree we had it pretty sweet. I smile at her then look back at computer. I was busy trying to finally pick a house Hero and I will purchase. As I am searching, all I can hear are Angela's six-inch heel knocking against my granite floor. "Angie, don't you have work to do girl, I am trying to pick out this house. If you will not help me do that, then go make noise in your own office." I cut my eye at

Angela, who puts her hands on her hips as she stands up and walks around the desk to have a look at the computer. I turn it so she can get a better view.

"I do not see the problem, I see at least four beautiful houses, Karla. Oh, maybe I will move next to yours, depending on which house you choose." I roll my eyes at Angela, as I see the one I want. "Angie! There it is! It's a six-bedroom, five baths, with three fireplaces, vaulted ceilings and bay windows. It has a fenced-in backyard and look at the size of it! Now we can own a dog!" Angela looks at it with confusing. "Girl what in the hell do you need with all those rooms. I mean it's just going to be you, Derius, Ayia and the little one. Why not a four bedroom instead?" I roll my eyes at her as I explain, "Angela, now you know my mom is our babysitter. Derius and I both agreed when we got a house we would have a room made up for when she is too tired to drive home to daddy or when they both want to stay over. Then during the holidays everyone can stay at our house instead of getting hotel rooms." Angela says she agrees with me. So, I call the realtor to set up a showing of the house, they tell me they can't show it till next week which is fine.

After setting the appointment for Wednesday, I excuse Angela out of my office so I can finally get work done. I get about four emails from Daryl, asking for documents and asking me bugging questions about my day. I ignore all those emails as I text Hero while he is at school. He reminds me that his game starts at eight pm and I should not be late. I promise that I will not be delayed as I look at the time. I take off early so I can get Ayia dressed to go her daddy's game. I say goodbye to Angela and head home. As I am driving home, I get a call from Daryl. "Hello. Mr. Dewight." Daryl laughs slyly at me. "Come on, Karla, we are not strangers. You do not have to talk so formally." I am not getting in this conversation with him. "Mr. Dewight, we are in a business relationship, and would like to keep it as professional as possible. If you do not mind."

Daryl annoyingly breathes into the phone. *I know he is pissed off at my answer, tough he will get over it.* "Well, I will not argue with you Ms. Jacobs…" I interrupt him before he can finish that sentence, "Mr. Dewight, I have told you many times I am a married woman, and that my last name is Phillips." I can hear him grinding his teeth this time. *Oh yeah, he is really pissed now.* "Ah yes, my bad a mere mistake, but things could change that fact Mrs. Phillips." There he goes again thinking he has all the cards in his hands. "I am sorry Mr. Dewight, but did you have a business oriented question to ask me? I am headed home to get ready to go to my husband's basketball game." This makes Daryl bust out laughing completely. I have to move the phone from my ear a moment. "A basketball game. Little Derius is on the team huh!?! Do you video tape him too, Mom?! Karla that is just too much, you are too grown to be attending college basketball games. Let alone to have a player on it!"

Rolling my eyes at this arrogant asshole, I have to say this: "aw, what's the matter Daryl, are you jealous, because Derius has more talent now than you did then? Oh wait! I'm sorry did it deflate your ego. I have to go, my star player is waiting on me and I can't keep him waiting because unlike you, I'm his number one fan!" Daryl is steaming mad now as he takes the phone from his ear but I can still hear him cursing. I hang up the phone and have a good laugh. I feel fantastic after saying that. I finally make it home as soon as I walk in my mom is pushing towards my bedroom. She doesn't let me kiss my little girl or anything. I walk into the room, and just smile. My Hero has roses on our dresser and on the bed matching college jerseys for Ayia and me. On the back of mine it says Beautiful and Ayia's says Princess. I check the time.

Oh shoot, talking to that idiot and fighting traffic it's already six-thirty pm. I quickly hop in the shower. I get Ayia and I dressed and we are off to Hero's game. We make there about ten minutes early. I have just enough time for Hero to give me a quick kiss before heading on the court. The game is amazing, Hero is killing the shots out there and I see everyone cheering his name. I am so proud of him, Ayia is screaming for her daddy. She loves when her daddy has the ball and when he makes a shot, which is every time. Soon the game is over and the Dawgs have won! Derius is the star of the game, he smiles up in our direction. Ayia calls out to her daddy as Hero waves up at us. We wait for Derius outside when we see

Franco and Shatoya. "Hey Shatoya! Franco!" I scream for them to come over. They come across and Franco takes Ayia. Ayia loves her Uncle.

Franco gives Ayia a big hug, as I talk to Shatoya. "Girl, you were amazing tonight!" Shatoya, shrugs a little as she holds her stomach. "Thanks, I am super hungry right now." Just then my little man inside of me, has the same reaction. "So am I girl, Derius better hurry up so we can eat." As I finish that sentence, I see Hero running towards us. "Franco! Man, I was waiting for you to come, that's what took me so long, Beautiful." Franco points at Shatoya explaining that he had to get Shatoya first. Ayia reaches for her daddy, in Franco's arms. Franco frowns up at Ayia. "Oh, so now you want your daddy, huh. Just throw your Uncle to the side, huh, Princess Ayia!" Franco blows into Ayia neck, she giggles and laughs as Franco give her to Derius. Derius puts Ayia on his shoulders wrapping his hand around her back to support her. "Ayia, did you enjoy daddy's game?" Ayia screams out "Yes!" as Derius laughs at her. "Do you want daddy to get you a basketball." Ayia screams yes as Derius laughs excitedly. "Okay Princess, Daddy will get you a basketball. Then Daddy can teach you how to dribble and shoot too, just like Daddy."

We all go out to eat, Shatoya starts feeling sick and goes to the restroom. I go with her as soon as she throws up. I have to throw up right after her. "Shatoya, when was your last period? Shatoya thinks about it for a minute, she then looks at me. "Karla, I had a period last month. It's too soon for this month though. I must be getting sick, I don't usually do that during the winter months. I usually get sick in the spring though." "You got a point Shatoya, but I would take a test just in case. You look like me when I get morning sickness or sometimes all day sickness, ugh." Shatoya looks at herself in the mirror, then rubs her stomach. "Karla, do you really think I might be pregnant for real? If that is true, I wonder how Franco would take it? You know he is such a big spoiled baby himself." I stand next to Shatoya, and smile as I hug her shoulders, look into the mirror with her. "I really believe that Franco would be just as excited as Derius was when he found out I was pregnant with Ayia. Even though Franco acts like he is hard most of the time, he still takes his cues from Derius. So, if you are that will be the best present you will ever give him."

Shatoya's eyes water up as silent tears fall from her face. She turns and hugs me tightly still crying. "Karla! I hope I am! I hope I am pregnant, I know that may sound stupid because I am in school, but you just have no idea what this will mean to me. I was abandoned as a child, by mother who I haven't spoken to in years. I was a ward of the court of Florida off and on until I was eighteen. Franco is the first man to ever really love and care about me. I know I am crazy, and all but Franco loves me, he respects me. He is the one who got me through high school and has pushed me to go to college! If I am pregnant with his child, I would have repaid him back with the most important and precious part of myself." I pull back from Shatoya. I never knew she had lived such a hard life. Shatoya is always a ray of light, who knew that light burned so bright from all that darkness in her past.

"Shatoya, I know that would make Franco so happy. He would be over the moon. You should take that test, but do not be disappointed if you are not. You and Franco have a lifetime ahead of you both." Shatoya smiles, hugs me again. We part from each other, I tell her to fix her face before we go back out. "Karla, will you go with me to go buy the pregnancy test?' I nod that I will go with her. "Of course, I will, I am here for you too Shatoya." We go back to our table, where Franco is losing his mind trying to figure out what is taking us so long. Franco asks Shatoya if she is okay, she kisses his cheek as she nods yes. Derius looking over at me, as I walk over to him. Derius kisses my cheek softly. "Beautiful, are you okay? Do you want some water?"

I smile at Derius as we finish our dinner with Franco and Shatoya. We go home to put our little Princess to bed. Derius is walking in the bedroom. "Oh Hero, I have set our appointment to look at the house next Wednesday." Derius thinks a moment to himself, then snaps. "I have class that day, pre-finals lecture, but once I am done. I will meet you there, just text me the address." Derius then hops in the bed with me, and cuddles with me till I finally fall to sleep. The rest of the week is spent getting ready for Christmas. These months have flown by ever since we got married. I do not remember much about Thanksgiving, we didn't do much this year trying to get ready for baby number two. Derius preparing for school and me trying to organize our lives with another baby on the way was taking a toll on me. If we could land this house before Christmas, we could give Ayia a Christmas she would never forget. Derius wants to play Santa Claus this year for Ayia. *But first thing is first, we have to get this house!*

The following Wednesday arrived quickly. I am at work, trying to clear up
some paperwork for Daryl before I go to my appointment. Angie walks in as I am busy trying to get these stupid reports finalized. "Karla, girl stop doing that for now and let's go to lunch." I laugh at my crazy friend. "Angie, did you forget what today is? I have that appointment to look at the house today remember, I have to finish this up before I go. I will not be back after I look at the house." Angie pouts at me, then kicks the door frame. "I wanna go to lunch, who will go with me now?" I laugh, then an idea, comes to mind.

"Angela, how about I text Derius and get Dexter's number for you and you ask him to lunch." Angela looks over at me with an *I KNOW YOU JUST DIDN'T* in her eyes. I shrug my shoulders, laughing. "Not a good idea?" Angela walks over to my desk, placing her newly painted nails on top of my desk.

"Now Karla, what do I look like asking a guy to have lunch with me, huh? Have Derius give him the hint that he should ask me out." I can't help laughing at her as I agree with her. I take out my cell phone, texting Derius. "Hero, the house address is at 0103 High House Drive, Powder Springs. Oh, do me a favor, tell Dexter to ask Angie on a lunch date today. Love you Beautiful." A few minutes later, Derius replies back to my message. "Okay Beautiful, I will be there right after class. Dexter should be calling Angela now, lol he sounds so excited. Love you more, Beautiful." I look up at Angela and wink at her, she gives me a weird look then her cell phone rings. She looks at it, she thumbs me up then walks away. I finish up the last report. *FINALLY!!!* I get my things together, getting ready to head out, when I see *him* walk into my office.

"HELLO KARLA!" I roll my eyes as Daryl struts into my office.

"What are you doing here, Daryl?" He smiles, then hands me a bag. It's black with silver sparkles on it. I take the bag, then look inside of it, *it's a Coach Bag!* I look up at Daryl, placing the purse back in the bag and slide it back over to him. Daryl doesn't get to say a word before Angela barges in the office. "Girl! Karla look at what Daryl got us." I blink twice, as Angela tells me how Daryl got all the ladies up front Coach Wallets and us Coach Bags. I stare at Daryl as he smiles at me, then says. "Karla, I was just congratulating the Atlanta Office on a wonderful first month. You really have it together here, Karla and I just wanted to thank you and your wonderful staff is all." Angela nods as she hugs her new red Coach Bag. I reopen my bag, removing the black Coach bag. I had to admit it was a very nice bag.

I shake my head, looking at my watch. "OH MY GOD, I'M GOING TO BE LATE!" I grab my things, running out of the bank. Daryl is fast at my heels as he grabs my arm.

"Karla, I was thinking we could have lunch." I have no time for him as I snatch away as I run over to the car. "NO!!! DAMN IT!" I am having the worst luck ever. My car has a flat tire! Daryl looks at the car then shakes his head. "Did you have somewhere important to go?" I look at him annoyingly. "Yes, yes I do. I have a viewing of a house I am buying in like an hour and I was heading over early so I would not be late." I watch as Daryl takes out his cell phone and makes a call. After a few minutes, he gets off the phone then walks towards his car. I huff as I look at the damage, then pull out my phone. Daryl calls me over to his car, I walk over to him still looking for the phone. "Get in." Daryl opens the passenger door for me. "No, Daryl that is not..." He cuts me off as he shakes his head, leading me towards the door. "Yes, it is. You have a flat tire, I called my maintenance people to come, get your car and replace the tire. I will take you to your appointment so you are not late. Okay?"

I look at my cell phone it was time for me to be on the road. A ride couldn't hurt, and I am running late. "Okay Daryl and Thank You." So, Daryl drove me to my appointment to see the house. I meet with the realtor Connie Shields, a pretty African American female, with green contacts. "Well Hello. I'm Connie Shields. It's so good to finally meet you Mr. and Mrs. Phillips." Daryl cringe at the sound of being mistaken for Derius. "No Connie, this is just my boss. I had some car trouble before I got here and he gave me a lift here." Connie looks at us, then shrugs at us. "Really, such a pity too, you too make an excellent couple." Daryl wraps his arm around my shoulder, pulling me in close to him. "You see Karla, even Connie, can see I am the man for you." I laugh as pull away from him, looking at Connie. "My husband will be shortly." Connie doesn't say anything as she shows me the beautiful house. I love it. "I can tell by looking at you Karla, you love it!" Daryl is impressed as well, as he looks around "Karla, I love this! You are going to have help me find my house, when I move to Atlanta." I look over at him in completely shock. "What do you mean, when you move to Atlanta?"

Daryl looks outside of a bay window. "Just like I said, when I move to Atlanta next month. We are building a corporate office and I have to come and oversee it." I sigh deeply,

I did not want to deal with Daryl's emails and phone calls let alone him soon to live in the same state! Daryl looks over me with that half seductive look in his eyes. "You know Karla, had things worked out between us, I would have loved to have bought you a house like this. You have always deserved the best, in my eyes at least." He is something else, he truly is. I walk over to Daryl, standing in front of him. Just as I am about to say what is on my mind. I hear Connie talking to someone. I follow her voice till, I find her. "I'm sorry young man, but there is no loitering on this property. I will have to ask you to leave, please."

My eyes are wide as I look at the priceless expression on Derius's face! He smiles, looking over at me. Connie looks behind me as I look at her. "I'm so sorry about this Mrs. Phillips. I will take care of this, give me a minute." I just nod as she turns back towards Derius who is now walking into the living room. "Young Man! You can't just walk around in here!" I giggle as I follow her into the living room. Connie is still trying to kick out Derius. He is loving every minute of this as he continues to walk through the house with her at his heels. Derius is too fast for her as she literally has to run after him. She misses him as he walks out of the kitchen and up the stairs. "Young man now, I have tried to be nice…. she stares at me, then looks around. "Again, I am so sorry Mrs. Phillips, I will get him out in a second. Did you see where he went?" I nod as I point upstairs. I attempt to finally tell her but she asks me to wait a minute, then darts up the stairs after Derius.

I walk up the stairs myself as I hear conversation coming from our soon to be bedroom. I open the door to a tense situation. Derius standing face to face with Daryl! It looks like I came in at the tail in of conversation. Just as I am about to say something to them, Connie finally catches up with Derius "OKAY YOUNG MAN, THAT WILL BE QUITE ENOUGH! If you do not leave right now, I'm calling the police." Derius smiles at Connie, then looks at me. "You are right that will do it, it's a wonderful house. Don't you think so, Beautiful?!" Connie blushes a little, thinking that he is talking to her. "Well, young man, I do, but I believe Mrs. Phillips here is going to buy it." I blush being called by my married name. Daryl has this annoyed expression on his face as he stares at Derius. "Oh, I agree with you, she should buy this house. Don't you agree Mrs. Phillips?"

I smile so big I think, I will blush to death. Daryl stares out of window with a rather piss off look on his face. I can't take it anymore, as I run over to Derius and plant a kiss on his lips. "Yes, I agree; we should buy this house, Mr. Phillips." A gasp from Connie's lips, "Mr. Phillips?" Connie stares at Derius, as he walks over to her extending his hand. "Yes, I'm Derius Phillips. I am her husband." Connie looks at me, as I hug Derius. "I am so sorry, Mr. Phillips, is it? " Derius nods then looks back at Daryl, who has had enough as he excuses himself. I follow him outside. "So, Karla, that is your little college boy huh? Well he is here now, I am sure that young Darius can get you home safely." I shake my head as I call out to him while he is getting in the car. "It's Derius and my HUSBAND can get me home, thank you, Daryl." Daryl gets in the car and speeds off. I laugh it off as I remember I left the poor woman with Derius alone.

I walk back in the house and find them standing outside in the backyard. Connie looks different as she is impressed with Derius's charm. I walk over to him, linking my arm in his. "So, you do like it, Hero?" Derius leans down kissing my forehead. "Yes Beautiful, I do like it. So, Connie, I believe we will take it." Connie beams with happiness. "That's great so now all I need to do is to send you the paperwork to apply for it. We finish up with Connie, and then head to the car. Soon as we get in Derius smile slightly disappears. "Beautiful, why was that man in the master bedroom?" I sigh knowing he already knew who Daryl was. "Hero, I got a flat tire and Daryl offered to bring me to the house showing so I would not have to reschedule." Derius's expression was not a happy one but one of being really annoyed to piss off. "Did he say something to you, when you two were in the room, Hero?" Derius shakes his head, as he composes himself. "Nah we just introduce ourselves that is all." I do not believe him, but then Derius looks at my bag.

"Wow Beautiful, I like your new bag, when did you buy it? Today?" I look down at the Coach bag that Daryl bought me today. "No, Daryl brought it when he came into the office today." I watch the muscles in Derius's face tighten. "He bought that for you?" I knew I had to diffuse this situation quickly. "Now, Hero before you lose it, he bought all the ladies a reward for having a great first month. All the tellers got coach wallets. Angie and I got bags." Derius stops at a red light, then turns to me. "Oh, is that right, well at least you are getting something out of all your work, huh, Beautiful? I am so proud of you." Then he kisses me softly, then passionately. I wrap my arm around his neck and kiss him back. The sound of a car honking brings us back to reality as he smiles at me, throwing his hand up to the driver in back of us. We get back to the bank and my car is there. It looks different though, as I look at the rims on the car with four new tires and it's been detailed and wax! Derius stares at the work, then at me. "Hold on Hero, let me go in and get the keys."

I run inside looking for Daryl but he is not inside. I see Angela getting ready to go home. "Angie, girl did you see my car outside?! Did Daryl come back here?!" Angela smiles really big as she winks at me. "Girl, that slick mother fucker did that car right. He didn't come back though. The guy who worked on it left your keys with me. Here you are girl. I have to go, I have a dinner date with Dexter." I take my keys from her. We walk back outside where Derius is standing in front of the car. "You said you had a flat tire not a pimp my ride makeover?" I laugh even though I can tell Derius is pissed off. "Hero, I didn't ask for this. I will have a talk with Daryl tomorrow, okay? I mean look at it." Derius shakes his head, then walks over wrapping his arms around me. "You like it don't you?" *HELL YES!* I was screaming in my head, but I knew it wasn't right. I kiss Derius on the cheek and he nods letting the situation go. I get into my car with new pimped out chrome rims and a new stereo system and head home for the night.

When I get home, I tell my mom about the house and show her my new Coach bag I got. After having dinner and feeling like a full cow. It's finally time for bed and Derius cuddles tightly with me. "Beautiful, promise me something okay?" As I lean deeper into his arms. "Yes, Hero what is it?" Derius looks down at me, kissing my nose gently then stares into my eyes. "Do not change on me,

Beautiful, stay the same woman I am still falling for." Tears build up in my eyes as I lean up to kiss Derius. "I promise, Hero, I will forever remain the Beautiful you love and adore." Derius squeezes me tightly as he falls asleep. I think about all that had happened today. No wonder he feels that way. Daryl had crossed a line with me today. But the things he had done were not all that bad. Nothing sexual or totally inappropriate. Soon I was in la-la land myself with this little baby kicking me.

***

Soon it was going to be Christmas Day and we had just got the house! Yes, we were in the middle of moving and decorating our new home. Derius, Franco and my dad were busy putting up the tree. My mom and I were shopping for stuff for the house and Christmas gifts for Derius and Ayia. I had bought so much stuff by the time Christmas came. Christmas Day in our new house is great. Everyone came over to the house. At Dinner Angela asked when I am going to have a baby shower. I have not even thought about it. "I guess after we find out what we are having." Franco looks over at Shatoya, who smiles at me as she stands up. "Speaking of baby showers, it looks like you will have to throw me one, Karla." Franco's face is priceless as he jumps up hugging Shatoya. He kisses her, then tears up. "I didn't even know." Franco laughs as Derius and Dexter hug him. Shatoya laughs hugging me tightly. "I am so happy Karla, I am so excited." I had to agree with her as she turns back to Franco. Franco composes himself, shaking his head. "Now, that is not what I thought Shatoya was going to tell you. I thought she going to tell you guys that we got engaged this morning." Everyone yells in excitement at Franco as Derius grabs him hugging him. We all watch the two brothers, in their moment. Franco can't help but cry because he didn't just become a soon to be husband but a father too.

As we are all in the living room talking about babies and watching T.V. Derius reminds me that soon it will be Ayia's first birthday. "Beautiful I am thinking of a Princess theme party for Ayia's first birthday, what do you think?" I agree with him, when my phone rings. "Hello." The voice on the other end brings me to roll my eyes. "Hello Karla, Merry Christmas." I am instantly annoyed hearing his voice on my phone. "Merry Christmas to you too, Daryl." Daryl laughs out loud, then sighs. "Well it sounds like you are busy, your Christmas present should be there in a minute, I hope you do like it. See you in the office on Monday." I simply hang up the phone. I takes me a minute to comprehend what he just said but then I gasp as I hear the doorbell ring. Derius looks at me then gets up to get the door, with me at his heels. Derius opens the door, a man in black suit is standing there.

"Is this the Karla Jacobs residence?" Derius sucks his teeth as she corrects the man. "Huh, this is Karla Phillips residence." The man looks at the box then shrugs at Derius. "Is Ms. Karla available to sign for this package?" Derius is about to snap when I walk in front of him. "I'm Mrs. Karla Jacobs Phillips." The man gave me the box and left. I just closed the door and went back into the living room. I sat next to my mom as I open the box. A loud gasp escape my lips as I look at the stunning diamond necklace in the shape of a heart. Derius walks over to me look at it, then me.

He looks so pissed off, as he walks away. I find the card; the gift is from Daryl. My mom just gave me an evil glance as I put my hands up in defense as I whisper to her. "I am giving it back mom." My mom gave me a look that could have killed me then and there. *I cannot believe this asshole sent this to my house!*

For the rest of the night things were quiet, Derius didn't say much and I can tell he was trying to play it off. Once everyone had left and we were in bed I knew I needed to talk to him about this. "Hero, are you asleep?' Derius didn't move really but shook his head. "Hero, I just want you to know that I am giving that gift back okay?" Derius turns and looks at me, pulling me close to him. "Beautiful, you know I trust you right? But I do not trust that guy. I mean what man sends another man's wife a present like that? He is your boss so I am going to let you deal with that. So, if you say you are going handle it, then I am going to let you handle it." Kissing him on his nose and cuddling up to him, my heart is finally at ease that Derius did trust me to take care of this. I went to sleep, determined that tomorrow I was going to tell Daryl off for good. Unfortunately, when I went to work the next day Daryl had left for New York and wouldn't be back any time soon. I was happy to know that he was gone too. That man was working my last nerve, with all his little antics. Now I could focus on Ayia's birthday in February and Derius's Championship game in March.

Time seems to fly by as we rolled into the New Year with an epic party at the house. Shatoya and I were talking baby names and genders of both of our babies. Even though she was only two months along, it is never too soon to think of those things. As for me, it was rounding the time to find out what we were having. Dr. Gray had some distressing new for me when I went to the doctor. "Mrs. Phillips, your blood pressure is a bit high, and you need to watch being overly active. Make sure you are resting properly." With all of the moving around, working, attending Derius's games and the stress I am going through with Daryl. No wonder I was feeling sluggish lately. After assuring Dr. Gray, I would rest; I went home. I am not going to tell Derius or my mom about this. All it will do is make the both of them worry like crazy about me. As soon as I got home and made sure everyone was good, I went to take a nap.

When I finally wake up, Derius was home from school and work. We didn't talk much, mainly because he had homework to get to. I didn't bother him and just let the week roll by me. No word from Daryl, I was so happy about it. Till the following Monday. I am at work, going through paperwork when I hear a knock at my door. I smile as I look up at the door, then my smile vanishes. "Daryl." I am not in the least bit happy to see him at all. "Don't be that way Karla. I need you to come with me right now, though." I roll my eyes as I inquire what it is he needs. "Well, I am finally moving to Atlanta this week. I need you to look over the new building with me because you will be managing that property's tellers there as well. You might even have to move to the main office." Well at least it's about work, so I collect my things and get in the car with Daryl. We do not really talk on the way there. Daryl gets a phone call, he is not on long, as I listen to the radio.

We continue to drive, when I suddenly realize as we turn into a parking lot; then park, we are not at the new building but a house! *Where in the hell has he brought me!?!* I turn to look at Daryl, who has already gotten out of car and is walking toward the house. I didn't want to get out car, but I really didn't have a choice. As I walk into the huge beautiful house. I am in love with the inside of house. I walk slowly through the house looking at the marble floor, vaulted ceilings, huge dining hall and the commercial size kitchen. I finally find Daryl talking to a man in the living room. I wait for them finish, then I walk over Daryl asking angrily: "Why are we here? I thought we were supposed to be looking at the new company office?" Daryl smiles slyly at me than saying coolly. "Yes, we were, but my realtor called saying that I could see this house that I am interested in. I decided to come see it and I knew you would tell me if it was me or not. You are not mad at me are you; for wanting your opinion on the house?"

I just stand there a minute not able to say too much of anything. He did just want my opinion on the house. I am mean he did give me his opinion of my house when I bought it. So, I continue to look at the house with Daryl. When we enter the backyard all I could do is gasp. It was huge, the realtor told us that Daryl could build a swimming pool easily out there. We finish looking at the house, Daryl tells him he will take the house. I walk back to the car and get in. Daryl came out shortly after and got in. We start driving again, as we are leaving the house. I get a text from Derius. I smile from ear to ear as Hero asks about my day and tells me he will be home late from practice. I put my phone in my bag and look at Daryl who is staring at me. "Was that your little boy checking in?" I raise an eyebrow at that arrogant prick. "Boy? Daryl just stop it will you?! Stop call him that! Stop with that condescending tone that you have whenever you mention him. Get this straight no matter how it makes you feel, Derius is MY HUSBAND! You will respect that or we will not have any form of conversation outside of business. Do I make myself clear?"

Daryl stares at me a minute like he doesn't recognizes me. Then he laughs, shaking his head. "My Karla is really all grown up, huh? Okay, okay my bad about your 'Husband', but Karla you have to feel me when I say this. I never once saw you loving anyone other than me. Now, I know what you are going to say but hear me out. I know I was distant in college, I was working toward a goal baby. A goal that you now see came true. You know my dad talked about wanting to run a bank all his life till he died. So, I had to make sure that his dream came true. Then on top of that, I met a woman who had the same dream, so beautiful, hardworking and had patience with me. I know that I was hard to deal with and you did it. I was proud to have you as my girl, Karla. Even after you broke up with me. I was even more determined to make your dream come true. I gave myself a deadline to make it and if I didn't I would just come running to beg you to marry me. When I had finally made it and all my dreams were real, I came to find you."

All I can do is stare at Daryl. We have finally made it to the new office building and are in the parking lot. Daryl puts the car in park as he keeps talking. "Only to find out that not only was I a year too late, but that the woman I was still in love with had a kid and was married. How do you think I felt to know that? I worked so hard to make all this possible for us. I wanted to give you results not just dreams. Now what am I supposed to do with this heart that only belongs to you? To see you with a guy that isn't up to your potential. To see you with someone else, yeah, I am jealous. I hate the thought he is the one you love, he is the one who gave you a child and he is the one who took my place." I have nothing to say at all, I never once thought Daryl worked so hard just for me. I thought he was doing it all for himself and his ego. This whole time, he did everything he did to make sure I would be happy. Tears fell slowly from my face as I take in Daryl's words. I finally look up at Daryl. He is crying too, he tries an attempt to compose himself but fails as he falls on the steering wheel.

We both cry in silence for a while, then attempt to return back to our reality. "Daryl, I am so sorry that you hurt this bad. I didn't know you did any of this just for me. I guess if things were different, I could say that I should been more patient with you. I should have believed in you more. But things are different now, I am married with a kid and one on the way. There is nothing I can do to change that now Daryl. I am sorry." Daryl nods at me as he looks at me. "How did you end up with him Karla? I mean let's be real, he is not really your type. So, I am very curious how this marriage even came to be?" I tell Daryl the story of how I and Derius met. I tell him about how he had saved me and how our roller coaster of a love life began. I tell him about everything that we went through. By the end Daryl is just staring at me.

"Karla, baby, you have been through so much! I never thought you would go through something like that. But after listening to you, I see how you could. Karla, you do know the reason you fell for him is that you were suffering from Hero Syndrome, right? I mean look at it, you were in a terrifying ordeal with begin mugged and scared for your life. This young man comes and saves you. You feel obliged to him and do things for him to show your gratitude that goes too far. When you went to jail, you had time to rationalize the situation, and you were coming out of it. But when you saw him again, the cycle started again. You felt you owed him the moon again. Karla by the time you realized your relationship with him was not for you and you wanted to move away; you found you were pregnant. Now you are pregnant, and you are thinking of your security. Karla, you did what anyone woman would do, secure a life for herself and her offspring. You made him take reasonability for placing you in that situation that resulted in you marrying him to ensure your child would be taken care of."

I thought a minute about what Daryl was saying. *Did I really stay with Derius because I was pregnant?! Was I suffering from Hero Syndrome, when I fell for Derius?! I mean to some extent it did make sense. I was an emotional wreck the whole time I was with him. I always had doubts about our relationship, the drama with his mom, and lastly the fact I didn't tell him I was even pregnant till we moved to Georgia. Did I really do all of that for us or was it all for myself?* I feel like an open book as Daryl shakes his head. I look down at my bag and out the window. "Daryl is that the reason I call Derius, Hero?" I look over at Daryl, who is shaking his head with his hand over his face looking up at the roof of the car. "Karla, yes this is why you call that boy Hero?! Yes, you were suffering from Hero Syndrome. I mean just look at you now. You still can't give a straight answer for your relationship. Plus, the Karla I knew was never this needy. You were always a confident, bold and a very independent woman."

I hate to admit it but Daryl is right. I was never a lost woman at all. I always strived for what I wanted and knew exactly what I was doing when I did something. Ever since I met Derius, I have not felt like that woman at all. Our entire relationship I could never really walk with confidence when I was with him. I constantly complained about the way people looked at us or felt about our relationship. I was always depending on Derius to get me through everything, even during our separation. I felt like I couldn't live without him. I was always wanting him to reassure me that he would be there. But I do love him that was not up for debate. Even if I felt this way, I still love Derius right? I look at Daryl and think about all the heartache I went through just to be with him. But in the end, I did cut him off and moved on. So, I was still in control of my life then, but now was I so sure I was that strong to do it to Derius.

Daryl leans in and gives me a hug, "Karla, you really should think about how you want your life to be. I mean you have a child and one on the way already. Are you willing to raise him into the man that is worthy of you? Daryl pulls back from me, looks me in eyes. "Should you even have to? Think about it really Karla. Is he your Hero or are you his? I mean you two are twelve years apart! How many years are you willing to wait for him to reach where you are now? Even if he does reach where you are now, let's face facts you will be too old to enjoy it with him." I know what Daryl is saying is true, but I am willing to try with Derius. "Daryl, I hear you and all, but I do love my Hero, and yes I am willing to see him make it to my level, because I love him." Daryl laughs at me, then looks sternly "Hero?! Besides that, one time he saved you, is he really a Hero or a headache? Karla that BOY cannot save you every time you need him to. If you lose your job tomorrow can he afford to support you, your child and that house. A house mind you that YOU bought! Can you name me anything in that house that he bought that matters?!"

The truth is besides a few little things, I have bought everything in our house. Derius just did not make enough money to buy anything, so I told him not to worry about it. Now he did help with bills, mainly the utilities but he did help out where he can. Hero is the nickname I gave him, it's the tattoo that I have that symbolizes him, but is Derius really my hero? I didn't want to talk about this anymore. I told Daryl to drop it and we finish looking at the building. Once we were done, he drop me off at my car at the bank so I can go home. He waited till I was getting inside. "Karla, I didn't mean to make you so upset earlier. I just had to finally tell you how I feel. I do still love you and care about you okay?" I just nod, get in the car and drive home. Some many things are on my mind right now, I cannot think straight as I drive home. So much has been revealed to me and I do not know how to process all of this. When I get home, I see Derius with Ayia in the living room. "Hey Beautiful, did you have a long day?" I sit on the couch and just rest as I stare at him. "Yeah Derius it was a long day, and I do not want to talk about it." I suddenly just get up and go upstairs to our room. That is how I ended that nightmare and fell asleep.

CHAPTER FOUR

THE GALA DRESS

I am playing with my Princess in the living room when Beautiful came through the door. "Hey Beautiful, did you have a long day?" Karla looked tired and worn out as she plops down on the couch. "Yeah, Derius it was a long day, and I do not want to talk about it." I had to do a double take when I heard the sentence. Karla just drags herself upstairs to our room. I give her sometime by herself. I went to check on her, she was fast asleep. She must have had a hard day. I really wish she would just sit down and rest, but how do you tell a busy woman with a bank on her shoulders to take a break. I have tried, I have pampered her when she was at her limit, but there is just so much I can do. Thinking about it now, I am reminded of what happened not too long ago when we were looking at this house. Walking around the house with that realtor chasing me trying to kick me out. Then I walk upstairs into one of the bedrooms there is a black man in a suit standing by the window.

"Ugh, excuse me but who are you?" The man in the suit turns slowly around looking at me. "Aw, you must be Karla's little college basketball player," I laugh to myself as I stare at this arrogant man in front of me. "Let me guess; you must be the worthless excuse of a man who could not keep Karla, huh?" The man smirked at me then adjusted his blazer jacket. "That was a nice try, but you forgot to mention that I am also the man who gave Karla her new job, huge salary increases and the money she is using to buy this house." I lean against the wall, smiling at this arrogant dick. "Well, while that all may be true, I am the man that Karla fell in love with. I am the man who is her lover, friend, father of her daughter and unborn child. Oh yeah did I introduce myself properly? I'm Derius Phillips, Karla's husband." I watch him frown up his face, checkmate. He exhales then shakes his head at me. "Yeah, you are, for the time being. I mean to tell you the truth I really do not know how Karla ended up with you. Young man, do not get me wrong you are a good-looking brother and all. But seriously what can you really offer Karla other than a dick?"

I had to admit I have thought about that many times in the time I have been dating Karla and after marrying her. How far apart we were in age, in our careers, and in our lives in general, but I was not about to tell this fool that shit! "Obviously I offer things you couldn't even begin to understand Daryl." Daryl raised an eyebrow at me, then walked towards me. I leaned off of the wall as we met in the room's middle. "Look here young man, I do not know where you get all your confidence from when you do not have a pot to piss in. See from where I am standing Karla doesn't have a man but another child she is raising on her own. I bet you can't even take her to the club or buy her a drink."

This man was really getting on my nerves. My face tightens all up a little, but I composed myself. "Why would I worry about things that do not concern me? Karla doesn't drink, she not a club person, so I will never have to worry about things like that." Daryl then looks down at his watch, then back up at me. "You think you have it all worked out don't you young man. But the truth is that you are lacking in areas you cannot even comprehend right now. For instance, can you afford this house if Karla lost her job tomorrow? Can you really stand there and honestly tell me you can take care of Karla? No, you can't. I can give and buy Karla anything she wants. It seems Karla only stays with you because she had no choice. She got pregnant, and she is not the type to do it alone. So that is where you come in."

My eyes narrow at Daryl, I had to admit that he had struck a vital nerve for a minute. I thought about all the issues I had with Karla in the beginning. All her doubt and constant emotional breakdowns, but then I thought about how together we overcame all of those obstacles. My eyes soften as I think about how Karla and I had made it through all of that together. How happy I am her Hero and her my Beautiful. When I thought about it that way, I regain my confidence. "My Beautiful is an amazing woman that is true Daryl. Karla deserves the world in my eyes. Yeah, you're right I am just an eighteen-year-old college student for now. Yes, Karla is ahead of me in her career and even in life, but even though she is so far ahead of me, she loves me."

"Karla is not a materialistic person at all. She has everything she ever wanted. She has the things YOU could never give her. She has someone who believes in her, who will fight for her, encourage her, and love her. Karla has a wonderful life, a career, friends, a family, a daughter who adores her, and a man… yes, Daryl a man who cherishes her with all I have in me."

Before Daryl could respond, Karla walked into the room. Staring at the both of us. Looking over at Karla now as she sleeps. I wonder to myself. *What has that asshole said to you Beautiful that makes you look so stressed out?* I put my Princess to bed and then her mom making sure they are both covered up and I kiss both them on their foreheads. I let the whole thing roll off my shoulders as I fall asleep. As time goes on and we round into the year two thousand and one, everyone stays busy. I do mainly because of school, basketball, work, and home. I tell Karla to take it easy at work because of the baby. She smiles sweetly at me. "I will Derius, don't worry." I give her a weird look as she hurries out of the door. Lately, I have noticed that Karla has been out later and later at night. I try to chuck it up to work, and doctor appointments. I have my own issues with going to class, playing basketball and working. I am completely exhausted but I have to admit, it's in a good way.

I finally felt like I was accomplishing my goals. Besides all of the school, and work. I am a great father if I say so myself. My little Princess will turn one soon in February, and Karla's birthday was coming around then too. At school, things are fine mostly, Franco seems more focused since he recently found out he is having a baby. While we were at practice, Franco is extra serious about getting things right. "DK man I am nervous. I didn't think we would have to think about kids till a year or two after we got married." I laugh at my crazy brother and best friend. "Life has a way of testing your true intentions when the time comes Franco. I know for sure it did for Karla and me." Franco passes me the ball as we are running drills. "Well, I have to agree with you there, you and Karla went through a lot of shit to get where you are now. How have you been with Karla working with that guy she used to date?" I feel the grip of my hands on the ball tighten as I almost throw the ball into Franco's chest. He catches it fast, but then stops and just stares at me.

"WHAT THE FUC… DK?!" I shake my head as I walk over to him. "SHIT! I am sorry Franco, but you just mentioning that asshole gets under my skin. Karla's actions lately have been bothering me too. She is coming home late, she always exhausted, and the worst of all she is calling me Derius." Franco raises an eyebrow at me as we walk to the showers. "DK isn't your name Derius? Why would you be concerned about that?" I cut my eyes at Franco. "What do you call me Franco?" Franco slaps me on the back, I wince from the stinging contact. "I call you a lot of names when you are not around me." Should I start there? He is trying to make me laugh, and it's working. I headlock him and spin him around for a few minutes.

Franco tries to get out of my grip as I playfully slap him on top of his head. "OH REALLY?! SO, YOU TALK SHIT ABOUT YOUR BROTHER WHEN HE IS NOT

THERE HUH?!" WHAT DO YOU SAY FRANCO?! HUH? HUH?" Franco is laughing too hard to respond. I finally stop and let him go. Franco rubs his head then punches me in the shoulder. "DK! MAN, YOU ARE MESSING UP MY HAIR!" Franco walks over to his locker, grabs his brush out of it then brush his hair in the mirror. "I call you my homie, my mentor, my friend, my partner in crime, my brother Derius and DK. I have a lot of names I call you and each means more than the next. So why are you mad that Karla calls you Derius when that is the name she fell in love with first?" I stare at Franco for a long time, this is the first time I had ever heard him make more sense than me.

"HOLD ON! Are you Franco Byars?! You are not my brother; my brother is not wiser than me?!" Franco finishes up his hair then looks over at me. "Well, I take my cues from you DK, so when I see you struggling on something. I usually just think about what you would say if it were me in that situation and it works out." I shake my head a minute, then slap Franco on the shoulder. "Nah?! Franco those words came from you. You are right

Franco, I am called by a lot of names and each one means more than the next. But there is one name I have come accustomed to hearing more than anything else. It is a name besides DK and Daddy that keeps my heart beating strong. I love hearing it so much and you do not understand how much I missed the sound of it when I was separated from Karla."

As we walk out of the gym, Franco nods at me. "I can understand why the name Hero means so much to you DK. It fits you perfectly, in every sense of the word. You should find out why she is not feeling like you match that name right now? Be mindful DK, she is pregnant again, she overworked and probably just exhausted." I sigh as we reach our cars and get ready to go home. "Yeah, I have thought of that, but I am missing something man. Karla is just acting distant more and more lately…. Franco cuts me off quickly "All right now, you two do not start this bullshit! You BOTH have a wedding to go to in like another what? Two and half to three months, so you and Mrs. Phillips need to get it together before then." Nodding my head, I understood what Franco was saying. I needed to just go home and talk to Karla. "I will man, do not worry we will be there together." Franco's eyes narrowed at me when he gets in his car and left.

No work for me today, I am going home to talk to Karla. I did not want to keep having this feeling of distance between us any longer. When I get home Ayia is playing with her toys and Mrs. Ellie is in the kitchen. "Has Karla come yet Mom?" My mother-in-law shakes her head at me as she stares at me. "Derius, son is everything okay?" I smile at her and nod my head. "Uh huh?! Derius Phillips, I have lived a long time on this earth son and I know when all my children are lying, even my son-in-law." I laugh, she is so right. She knew I was lying. "Okay Momma, I am not alright. Karla has been so stressed out and overworked lately. She has been so cold and distant to me too. I want her to talk to me about it, but she doesn't want to. What do I do about your beautiful, stubborn daughter Momma?"

Mrs. Ellie smiles at me then walks over and hugs me. I hug her back tightly, in that moment I really miss my mom. "Derius, you know about that snake name Daryl, right? I clear my throat as she says Daryl's name. "Yes, Ma'am I do." Mrs. Ellie nods as she releases me. "Daryl was Karla's first love and I believe Karla was his. He can't let go of the fact he lost her and now is showboating for Karla in front of you. Karla has never had all of this before. She was spoiled but humble always, but money and power can change a person Derius. Keep your wife grounded. Remind her of all the things she has that money can never buy son." I love this woman so much, in an instant she makes me feel I can conquer the world again. I give Mrs. Ellie another huge hug as I hear Karla coming into the house.

I excuse myself as I come out of the kitchen just in my time to see my wife walking down the hall towards our bedroom. I walk up behind her and wrap my arms around her. I can feel Karla tense up as I squeeze her tightly. "Am I a stranger to you now Beautiful?" Karla turns around looking at me with guilt in her eyes. "I'm sorry Derius, I have just been going through a long transition at the office, and this little guy inside me is not giving me much help." Once again, I hear her call me Derius, instead of Hero. I want to ask about it but right now my wife looks tired. I pick her up and try to carry her to the bed. Karla fights me to put her down. "DERIUS! THIS IS NOT FUNNY! I AM NOT IN THE MOOD FOR YOUR GAMES RIGHT NOW! I TOLD YOU I AM TIRED!"

I breathe in deeply trying to contain myself. "I know, that was why I wanted to carry you and put you to bed." Karla rolls her eyes at me as she undresses. "I just need some space is all Derius. I am too tired for your immature games right now okay?!" The look on my face is priceless, as I stand there with my mouth open. "Immature, huh?! So, me wanting to help you off of your feet is immature now?!" Karla rolls her eyes then looks up at me. "You are taking my words out of context Derius. I mean I am too tired to play with you right now." *I cannot believe this.* "Karla, are you being condescending to me right now? I am sorry if me trying to pamper my wife is childish and immature. Maybe I should be Daryl huh, uncaring and distant. Would you prefer that, huh Karla?!"

Karla closes her eyes, then breathes deeply. "Are you serious right Derius?! That is really mature to bring him up in this conversation that clearly has nothing to do with him. THIS has to do with YOU being a childish brat and having consideration for how I am feeling right now!" I laugh as I stare at Karla. "OH, NOW I AM CHILDISH BRAT?! Let me tell you something about this childish brat, huh. I am tired too, Karla, of you acting like a fucking victim all the damn time! It's not because you are pregnant either, it's because YOU can't make up your fucking mind what you want! You have everything you could ever want right in front of you, but no…! You are clearly thinking of all the shit you missed. Which when you think about it is not much. Oh yea, I have watched MY WIFE, become this distant, cold-hearted bitch I see before me…"

I feel it before I realize it. Karla slaps me across the face. In an instant, I know I deserved that slap. I grab her close but she fights to get out of my grip. I hold on tighter to her as she screams at me to let her go. "I'm sorry, baby! I am sorry Karla. I know I should never disrespect you like that, but baby you have to see why I feel this way. Where is my Beautiful at?! Where is the woman I am deeply in love with?!" Karla stops fighting me then hugs me tightly. I can feel my shirt soaking in her tears as I hug her tightly. Rocking her back and forth in my arms. I say nothing else. I let us have this moment of silence. As I listen to her cry, I think of how much I love this woman. NO matter, what I feel at this moment, I know ultimately, I love her.

Karla looks up at me then, shakes her head. "No more fighting, Beautiful, let's go to bed okay?" Karla hug me tightly again, then nods. We say nothing else the rest of the night. We get into bed and just fall asleep, no cuddling or anything. In the middle of the night, I wake up to silent tears. Karla is crying in her sleep. I roll over, hold her tightly and kiss her nose. She calms down some, then goes back to sleep. I look at her, there is something I am missing, or lacking in supporting her. I wish I knew what it was so I could see her smile again. For now, I will let it go and just be here for her. This is all I can do for her. I kiss Karla on the nose once more and fall asleep.

I let go of my nagging anger for now and concentrate on my Princess's birthday party. Ayia was finally turning one year old. Franco, Shatoya, Angela, and Dexter help with the decorations for the party. Karla, her mom, and my mom fix the food. Even though my mom is now confined to a wheelchair, she can still manage. Soon the party is underway. We have dressed our princess up in a custom princess gown. We have invited the kids she plays with from the neighborhood. They were asked to dress up too as princes, and princesses. She has on her crown, and wand, to complete the theme. Karla and I are dressed up at as king and queen. Ayia is blessing everyone, enjoying her snacks and gifts. We got her an outdoor playhouse for the backyard, a new doll with accessories and her first bike! Ayia is spoiled rotten as she opens all the rest of her gifts from everyone. Everything is going well, even Karla and I are playing around again. We stand next to each other laughing at the kids playing in the play bounce I ordered for this event.

Not long before Ayia is getting ready for her birthday cake, there is a knock at the door. Momma Ellie goes to open it and I can hear her in the hallway. "What on earth are you doing here?!" Everyone turns their heads to the sound of Momma Ellie's voice. Then my eyes narrow instantly as Daryl walks in the room. My eyes scan the room looking for Karla. When I finally locate her, she is just as amazed as me. Karla looks in my direction, shaking her head. "She didn't invite him?!" Is the facial expression she is wearing as I look back at Daryl. Daryl smiles at everyone, in the room. "Hello, everyone. Karla told me you were having a birthday party for Ayia today, so I thought I would drop by and give her a present."

Daryl's eyes met mine, his smile grows wider. I am about to say something when Franco grabs my shoulder. I look back at him; he shakes his head then nods at Ayia. She is beaming from ear to ear. The other guests there do not know about our situation and why should they? So, I keep a cool head, walk over to Daryl and extend my hand out to him. Daryl smirks as he grips my hand hard, I tighten my grip. "Thank you for coming Daryl, the refreshments are in the kitchen. We are just getting ready to cut the cake." I release his hand and walk over to Karla, wrapping my arms around her waist. Karla seems uncomfortable as she removes my arms from around her. She walks away from me and kneels next to Ayia as we sing happy birthday. The cake is cut and ice cream is handed out to everyone. I am standing by myself staring at Daryl talking to everyone there. I feel a hand suddenly on my shoulder.

I look back at my father-in-law Robby J. "Derius, I know what you are thinking son. I hate the bastard too. Daryl is the first man to break my little girl's heart. When she was in college, she came to me crying when she broke up with him. I do not understand why, he believes he can just show back up out of the blue and recapture her heart? I can see in your eyes you want to walk over there and punch him in the face, but I am glad you didn't make such a scene on your daughter's birthday." It's true I want to punch this arrogant asshole so badly, but this is my daughter's day and I will not ruin it. Daryl then screams for everyone's attention. "OKAY! EVERYONE, NOW I WILL REVEAL MY PRESENT TO PRINCESS AYIA!" He walks over to Karla and kneels down on one knee. "Queen Karla, will you assist me?" Karla smiles at him and nods.

It takes everything in me not to blow up. Robby J and Franco grab my shoulders. Ayia looks over at me with a smile and I smile back at my princess. Karla looks at me and I narrow my eyes at her. "I do not understand what in the hell she is thinking but once this party is over, I will FIND OUT!" That is all that is going through my head as Daryl and Karla bring in a very large box. Once they put it down. Ayia stands in front in awe. "Princess Ayia, it brings me great pleasure to present to you a carriage fit for a princess." Karla and Daryl then untie the ribbon and it opens to reveal a custom-made pink and purple BMW car! Everyone laughs and cheers for the gift. It amazes Karla and Ayia is over the moon.

I am done. I kiss Ayia then walk back to our bedroom. *This motherfucker! He just likes to one-up me at every turn. Even at my daughter's party*. I lie down on the bed and just try to take a nap to cool off my anger. Soon Karla comes back to get me to say bye to everyone. I walk back out to the living room and bow that the King is about to retire for the night. I thank everyone for coming and I go back to the bedroom. Soon I hear people leaving including Daryl. Karla puts Ayia to bed she has had a very eventful day. Just as I am finally about to drift off to sleep, I hear Karla come into the room. "Derius, are you asleep?" Again, with that name, I tense up every time I hear her call me that. For the past couple of weeks, that's all I have heard.

I pretend to be asleep; I do not want to talk about anything especially about Daryl. After that, I have been walking around in a void. It shows more when I am at home than at school or basketball practice. At work, it's all a blur and then I am back at home pretending once again. I notice the change in Karla. She is dressing more expensively. She is still calling me Derius, her actions are more demanding. Suddenly I have no idea who I have married. We do not talk, and if I attempt to, she blows me off and tells me I am acting childish. Each time makes us fight and go to bed mad at each other. No matter the fact, I still blame her pregnancy hormones for her actions. I keep a level head and keep loving and supporting her every move. I keep all these bottled up emotions inside me. I allow myself to take the brunt of her frustration and exhaustion.

This has been going on for another week. Karla's birthday is coming up soon, and I want to do something special for her. So, I plan something special for her. A couple of days before Karla's birthday she comes in the house with a box. I do not say much but when she goes to the bathroom. I look inside the box, inside is a white and gold gown, matching shoes and jewelry. I look further and see a card. I pick it up and read it. "HAPPY BIRTHDAY KARLA!! LOVE DARYL." I drop the card as Karla steps out of the bathroom. "Derius? What are you doing" I barely hear the words she is saying as the words on the card repeat in my mind, *Happy Birthday Karla! Love??? LOVE WHO? Not MY WIFE!?!* I look at Karla, rubbing the back of my head. "Karla, where are you going?" Karla looks at the box then back at me. "I have to attend a gala with Daryl to look for some new paintings for the bank."

"You have to attend a gala with Daryl? Karla, you have been going out late for past few weeks. Don't you think you should rest sometimes?" Karla looks annoyingly at me. "Derius, this is for my job. Yes, I have to go…." I cut her off quickly. "Do you even remember that you are pregnant, while you come strolling in the house late!?! You know it's not good for you or the baby, right?" Karla folds her hands in front of her and huffs. "Derius…." I lose it. I have to get this shit off my chest before I snap for real. "DERIUS?! WHO IN THE HELL IS DERIUS HUH KARLA?!" Karla laughs at me throwing her hands in the air. "Who is Derius? Are you serious; that's YOUR NAME! Derius Kenai Phillips!"

I walk over towards her standing in front of her, pulling off my shirt I reveal my chest and point at the tattoo over my heart. "THAT IS NOT WHAT YOU CALL ME! THIS IS WHAT I CALL YOU! BEAUTIFUL! NOT NE NE AND NOT KARLA! I CALL YOU BEAUTIFUL! But right now, I do not know who the hell you are!" Karla looks up at me like she is about to cry. I shake my head and step back. "Ever since this nigga has come back into your life, I watched you change. From that time, I walked into this house and he was here. When he bought you the Coach bag, pimped out your car, and that fucking necklace at Christmas. To make matters worse the motherfucker had the fucking balls to come to MY DAUGHTER'S birthday party uninvited and bring her that fucking car!" I look over at the dress, grab the box slamming it on the ground. "WHO IN THE HELL ARE YOU!?! BECAUSE YOU ARE NOT MY WIFE!"

Karla closes her eyes as I rage at her. When she opens her eyes; tears are flowing down her face. "Derius you are being really childish right now! Are you jealous of Daryl because he can do the things you can't do?" If I was not Alexandra's child I would have probably hit her. "CHILDISH?! JEALOUS?! Are you fucking kidding me right now?! Karla, you are MY WIFE! I am YOUR HUSBAND, NOT DARYL! I have a right to be pissed off about ANY MAN OTHER THAN ANTHONY AND YOUR DADDY buying you anything! Childish you say? Yea, I am for wanting to know why I am being such a punk and not snapping sooner about this bullshit! Yea for not busting that arrogant bastard in the face when he showed up at my door uninvited! Yea Karla, bet I am childish, for trusting that you had this shit under control! For trusting that my wife would not change on me, NO not my BEAUTIFUL! Because she is not that type of person! HELL, YEA I am childish!"

Karla just stares at me for a long time, shaking her head. "Derius…" I cut her off again. "STOP FUCKING CALLING ME THAT! Why are you acting like this!?!" I pause a moment, pacing the floor of our bedroom. Karla leans against the wall look up at the ceiling. "No, she cannot just stand there crying; and making me feel like I did her wrong here!" I walk over to her, grabbing her shoulders. "SPEAK! TALK TO ME! I am tired of keeping this inside me. I want you to explain why I am losing my wife NOW!" Karla looks up at me then breaks down, she sinks to the floor crying. I lean on the wall looking down at her. I try to get my anger together, but it's no use. I kneel looking at Karla, I had to hear this answer, even though I already knew why.

Karla looks at me with a tear-stained face. "I have been emotionally messed up lately. And then Daryl said…" I fall back on my butt, leaning against the side of the bed. "Daryl! Karla the only time you call me Derius, is when you doubted us. So, tell me this Karla. What is it that man could have possibly said to you to make you doubt me, the man you married?" Karla stares at me for several minutes. Closes her eyes, then sighs in defeat. "A while ago Daryl and I went to check out the new corporate building in Atlanta. We were in the car, and Daryl got a phone call, and then we went to look at his new house he moved into. Once we left there and finally got to the building. Daryl asked me how I met you, I told him the story of us. Once I finished, Daryl told me I had been suffering from Hero Syndrome."

I could not believe my ears. I coughed as I stared at her. "HERO SYNDROME?! So, the ONLY reason you fell for me is, that bastard said, you suffered from Hero Syndrome." Karla then looked down at her hands, she was shaking now. I went to touch her shoulder, but she shies away from me. "That's not it, Daryl talked about the reason I stayed with you even with being threatened with prison. He said I was suffering from Hero Syndrome, and when I got arrested I was coming out of it, but then I found out I was pregnant. He said I stayed with you because I was looking out for my own security." My mouth flew open as I stare at Karla, I jump up still staring at Karla. *THIS IS NOT HAPPENING RIGHT!?! Karla is not saying she believes that ASSHOLE?!*

I was developing a very large headache and his name is DARYL!! Suddenly, before I could control the level of anger I am expressing. "WHAT?! So, let me get this straight now, the ONLY reason you could have fallen for me is because you were suffering from Hero Syndrome! Then the ONLY reason to stay with me is that you got PREGNANT! So here is my question, Karla. Do you believe that?" Karla looks at me with apologetic eyes. The pressure I am feeling right now is like a heart attack, but it's just my heart breaking. "Karla please tell me that is not true." *PLEASE BEAUTIFUL, TELL ME YOU DIDN'T STAY WITH ME BECAUSE YOU DIDN'T WANT TO BE A SINGLE MOM! KARLA, PLEASE BEAUTIFUL, TELL ME THAT EVERYTHING THAT BASTARD SAID ABOUT YOU IS NOT TRUE!*

I am no longer in control of my emotions as tears erupt from my eyes. Stunned by the look on Karla's face. I beat my chest as my heart feels like it will lock up on me and just stop. "NO NOT MY BEAUTIFUL! SHE'S NOT THAT TYPE OF PERSON! NOT MY KARLA, SHE'S NOT MATERIALISTIC, SHE WOULD NEVER BETRAY ME, AND SHE LOVES ME! KARLA PLEASE TELL ME THIS IS NOT WHO YOU REALLY ARE?! PLEASE TELL ME I DIDN'T ALMOST LOSE MY MOTHER FOR YOU FOR NOTHING! THAT I DIDN'T GIVE UP MY WHOLE LIFE, SCHOLARSHIP, FRIENDS, EVERYTHING TO MOVE HERE WITH YOU! THAT EVERYTHING THAT PEOPLE EVER SAID ABOUT YOU AND I DEFENDED ABOUT YOU WAS NOT TRUE!" Karla is crying uncontrollably now, she is beating the ground. I fall to my knees, I can't control the tears. The pressure in my chest feels like it will explode.

"Hero Syndrome. When did I once say you owed me for saving you?! When did I once make you feel obligated to me?! I sit up point at my chest as I continue my rant. "THAT IS

NOT THE KIND OF PERSON I AM! THAT IS NOT THE PERSON MY MOTHER, ALEXANDRA PHILLIPS RAISED! Since when did I make you feel you owed me for being a good fucking person? Ever since he has come back in your life, you changed but why!?! When you didn't have this new position or the money we were happy. Is that what you want, do you want Daryl because he can buy you the world? Do you want a man who will buy you everything, then leave you alone? Someone who is so consumed with making money you spend no time with him at all? Then when he does something wrong he buys you gifts instead of saying 'I'M SORRY'?"

I finally calm down some as I sit on the floor with my head in my hands. "Karla, I know that I am only eighteen, but I thought you love me because of the things I do for you; not what I could not buy you. I may not be able to buy you the world, but at least I thought you knew you are my world. I will give everything I have and everything I will become to you. I thought you were happy to have a man, who pampered you himself, who encouraged your growth, who was not intimidated by your success. Who loves you with all of my heart and soul?!" I look up at Karla, the woman I love, respect and adore. She stares back at me, just as broken as I am. "Beautiful, I hate that I am yelling at you. I hate this man can do this to us, we have been through so much in three years. I have always looked at us like an epic love story that has yet to be written. We have been through so much that, NOTHING should be able to break us down. I guess I was wrong, huh?"

Karla shakes her head; the tears are still flowing heavily down her cheeks. She then crawls into my arms, and I hug her tighter than I ever had in my life. I let her tears soak my skin as mine fall on top of her head. For a minute we cry together. I love this woman; I do NOT want to lose her for no reason. Karla coughs and I pat her on the back. "Hero." The sound of her calling me that mends the pieces of my heart instantly. "Hero, that is not true, baby. Not at all when Daryl said those things I thought they might be true. He said I was not the same woman he knew. He mentioned that I used to be independent, strong-willed and I would never do anything without thinking. He asked me if you were my hero or was I yours."

I could understand to some extent why she would have a doubt with that question. *I still support her, but do I really possess the "HERO" factor as much as she always claims I do?* Karla's voice cracks through the tears, "I thought about it a lot lately. I noticed when I am with you I depend on you. You keep me grounded at every turn. Hell, when you were away, I could barely breathe without you. Then before I realized it I was doubting you again. I hated myself for that, so much I could not even look at you. How could I stand next to you knowing even for a minute I had doubted you again? That I had allowed another person to make me feel bad about the beautiful love that surrounds me. So yes, I stop calling you Hero, because I didn't deserve to when I am feeling this way."

I pull Karla back from me and stare at her. I shake my head then kiss her nose. Karla hugs me tightly as I caress her head. *MY WIFE* is all I can think of as my anger disappears. Karla had doubted me and punished herself because of it. "Beautiful, I am so sorry. I didn't know you were feeling…" Karla cuts me off with her finger against my lips, "No Hero, I am sorry. I have let all of this new fame and fortune get to my head. I allowed someone to come and try to destroy everything we have fought to have, and I am sorry for that. I will never ever doubt you or us again. I promise."

I smile as I pull my wife close. "Karla, Beautiful I know that there will always be times when you will doubt me. Hell, I am only eighteen years old. So, there will be times when I act like an eighteen-year-old. Like now, I should have asked you what you were going through instead of just yelling about how I felt. I know it was immature of me." Karla is about to say something when her phone rings. The phone is on the bed, I reach for it and see it's Daryl. I sigh as I hand her the phone. Karla looks at it then at me. She answers the phone call. "Hello, Daryl. No, I am not going. I have somewhere very important that I need to be." Karla hangs up the phone on Daryl and tosses it back on the bed. Then lies on my chest, I can do nothing but smile as I wrap my arms around my wife.

Yes, now that is MY Beautiful. We lie there in each other's arms until we fall asleep.

CHAPTER FIVE

WHEN THE BUZZER SOUNDS

Since Derius and I have talked it's very apparent I need to work to keep our marriage sound. No more being a weak person when people, including Daryl, mention my love for my husband. *Karla how could you even listen to him, even if he did work hard to be with you, would you leave Derius for Daryl?! HELL NO!* Just the thought of having to ask myself that question, tells me my feelings for Daryl have really affected the way I even see my OWN HUSBAND! Thinking back on that fact and looking at the heartbreaking expression on Derius's face almost killed me. Derius does his absolute best to be everything I dream of and what do I do?! I make him feel like the love he gives me is not enough. *YEAH KARLA! YOU DOUBTED HIM ONCE AGAIN*! Derius said it himself that he understands he is on a different path behind mine, but that he is willing to let me shine and push forward to reach me.

In some ways, Daryl is very much right. I have strayed from the woman I was in college. The woman I was in college would believe Derius more than anything. Now the Wife/mom/Branch Manager needs to do the same. In the beginning, it was out of fear of loving him too much and him disappointing me in the end. I was scared to give him everything because of my history with Daryl. Now because of Daryl, I feel bad because of him once again. No more. Either I am going to stand for my beautiful marriage or forever live in the past of love that could have been. I am going to march forward with my Hero. Yes, I am going to finally close the chapter of what could have been with Daryl. When I return to work, Daryl does not come by. Even as my birthday nears, I do not hear a word from him. I am happy that he does not either. My birthday comes before I know it. It falls on a weekday, so I am at work, mad of course. Derius tells me that we will celebrate it this weekend. I am working in my office when I see a delivery man enter my door. I motion for him to come in, he walks in with a huge bouquet of roses, for a minute I think they are from Daryl. I take the card out rolling my eyes until I read the card.

They are from Derius! It reads; "No matter, your age I will always be thinking you are the most Beautiful, Strong, Intelligent, and Emotional Woman, that I will FOREVER love with my ENTIRE HEART! HAPPY BIRTHDAY BEAUTIFUL! Love, HERO." I beam from my ear to ear. "Yeah, I am overly emotional, aren't I Hero?" I think to myself with a laugh. I sign for my flowers and arrange them on my desk before I can even sit down. I get a glimpse of a suit in my eyesight, and I sigh knowing it's Daryl. So, I sit up getting ready to give him an ear full. When I turn toward him, I am shocked it's not Daryl, but DERIUS! "HERO! What are you doing here?!" Derius pulls me close to him, then kisses me. Those soft, tender lips almost make my leg buckle under me. Derius grips me tightly to him as our kiss continues.

When he lets me go, I try to regain my composure. "Happy Birthday, Beautiful." I am all smiles, blushing from ear to ear. Only my Hero can do that to me. Only with him do I feel young and beautiful even though I know today I just turned thirty years old! "Thank you, Hero, now what are you doing here? Don't you have a class or practice today?"

Derius smiles at me as he grabs my purse and pulls on my arm. "Derius where are we going? I am not done with work." Derius pulls me in for another kiss. I can hear the tellers outside getting jealous. I push Derius back some. "Hero…." Derius cuts me off. "Beautiful, you have been working long hours in this office for months. Today is your birthday, come play hooky with me." I laugh at Derius, as I cut off my computer, lock my door.

I peek my head into Angie's office; she smiles at me as I wave to her. She nods as she waves at Derius, who gives her a wink. We walk out of the bank, get into Derius's BMW, his mom got him for graduation and rode off. Derius takes me out to eat, takes me to a spa and presents me with my birthday present at dinner. It's a beautiful heart-shaped diamond necklace. "Oh Hero, I love it!" Derius puts the necklace on me, kissing my neck. From another table, I can see a couple looking at us. I lean over the table and kiss Derius for a good thirty seconds. "Wow, Beautiful what was that for?" I laughed shaking my head at myself, yes, I am proud to be with this handsome man I call my Husband. "Are you excited about your big day, Hero?" Derius looks at me shaking his head. "Today is your day Beautiful, no talk about me, Ayia, the house, that job or that man."

I agree to not to talk about nothing ordinary. We enjoy dinner; it has been a wonderful day and early part of the night. Derius looks down at his watch, then at me. "Okay Beautiful off to the next event." I look at him with sheer confusion, what else is there to do at this time of night but go home. I do not ask just follow my Hero out and into the car. I am in awe as Derius takes me to a concert in the park. We sway to the music they play, dance under a tree with our shoes off. Soon it's time to go home, but Derius doesn't take me home, but instead to a beautiful hotel. As Derius lets me out of the car, he pops the trunk and pulls out two duffel bags. He has planned every detail, hasn't he? Once inside I realize this is the same hotel Derius stayed in when we were separated.

We reach our room, as Derius opens the door. I see the candles leading to the design on the bed. "Happy Birthday Beautiful" on it. I tear up as I look around the room. On the wall is a long timeline photo collage of me from birth till now. I cry as Derius holds me swaying me back and forth. He listens to me tell stories of each photo. When I am done, he spins me around then leans in for an intense kiss. "Beautiful, this is the room I was a prisoner in for the time frame we were separated. Tonight, I want you to live out a fantasy I have had since I was trapped here." I look up at him, remember this is also the room he almost had a threesome in, and where he fake slept with Jasmine in too. "What is your fantasy Hero?" He smiles as he walks to the window. "I want to make love to the reflection of you. I want to stare out this window and helplessly fall for you all over again." We did just that, and it was one of the best birthdays I had ever had. I was now stone solid in my marriage to Derius. Even though he may rub me the wrong way sometimes, he is still charming, and he is still my Hero.

***

March and spring is upon us. Derius has a championship game in the middle of the month. I have so much to do in a short period. The bank is having an audit soon, which means at least two late nights. I have explained to Derius these are one hundred percent mandatory. I know he is worried about the baby and me, but I promised to him I will be fine. Today has been quite the day as we get ready for the audit at work. Angie is busy getting files together, and I am working on organizing the team together for the auditors.

On top of that it's business as usual. Daryl has not shown his face since I hung up on him other than a few emails for business. And that is the best news I have experienced recently.

Angela walks into my office as I am getting ready for lunch. "Girl if you do not hurry up, we will NEVER eat." I laugh at my best friend as I close down my computer and grab my purse. Angela looks down at my bag. "Where is the Coach girl?" I shake my head, pushing her out the door. "I will tell you at lunch girl." We got lunch at a nearby seafood restaurant. "Okay girl, catch me up on all this drama." I shake my head; I do not want to bring up the past events, it has not been a month yet. "Angie, girl, I do not want to talk about it." Angela gives me the *Oh no miss thing, we are discussing this* face and now I have to tell her or she will kill me.

So, I go in with first with the things Daryl said to me at the new corporate building, then into explaining the drama at Christmas and Ayia's birthday party. I keep going on and on until I tell her about the fight Derius and I just had before my birthday. "KARLA! You mean to tell me you still have FEELINGS for Daryl?!" I had to admit to myself that I did, but those feelings were sort of out of guilt. "Yes, in a way, but the way it is because of all the beautiful things he told about working so hard for me." Angie shook her head in pure disgust. "Karla, girl, that boy may have had feelings for you, and frankly he still might. However, that does not excuse him in any size, shape, or matter that he ignored you. Supposedly Daryl was working for your benefit, so why was he engaged not once but twice in the time you have not been together?!"

I clenched my chest, "Girl, you better quit lying to me! Daryl was engaged!?!" Angela rolls her eyes at me then nods. "Girl, that stupid piece of a nigga was engaged to MY cousin. You remember Candice don't you from college?" I thought a moment; then I did recall a Candice, who called herself being pregnant by Daryl right before I finally dumped him. "Yes, I do recall your classless cousin." Angela agrees as she nods, then holds my hand. "Okay, so what I am about to say to is out of love, and do not get mad at me okay!?!" I stare at my best friend as she tightens her grip on my hand. "Uh huh," is all I could muster to say at the time.

Angie looks down at the table then speaks. "Candice and Daryl did have sex while he was with you. She told me everything, but what is worst Daryl begged me not to tell you." I snatched away from her, just staring at her. "Girl! You know what that shit is all in the damn past. I am past Daryl's ass now. I have Derius; I have my Hero! I was the stupid one to almost fall for one of Daryl's textbook lies again." I told Angela I did not want to talk about this anymore. We finish our meals, as we were leaving my phone rang. "Hello." rolling my eyes, it was Daryl. Speak of the devil, and I had conjured him up. "Karla, I saw that you are not in your office right now.

Could you come to the corporate building in half an hour?"

What does this man want now? I told him I would be there soon. I look over at Angela who is already shaking her head. "Please Karla do not fall for that bastard again, please." I hug my best friend, telling her that I won't fall for Daryl or his bullshit. I leave her and head to the corporate building in Atlanta. As I walk in, I see Daryl talking to the security guard. He sees me, motioning me toward him. I walk towards him, once next to him. "What can I do for you, Mr. Dewight?" Daryl gives me a concerned look as we walk towards the elevator. "Mr. Dewight, huh? Okay, Ms. Jacobs…" I cut him off quickly, "Mrs. Phillips. Mrs. Karla N. Phillips." Daryl shakes his head while he laughs me off.

"Anyway Karla, I asked you here to see how you are coming along with getting ready for your first audit." I roll my eyes at him. *I mean, is all he wanted? Hell, he could have asked me that over the phone.* We walk into Daryl's office; he has me have a seat. "Karla I am serious here. I take my business very seriously. Please do not think that because my feelings are still there for you, I would allow any harm to come to my business. Do you understand?" Was he implying I would not be prepared for the audit! *Boy, you better stop underestimating me.* "Mr. Dewight, I have worked for in the banking industry for as long as I have been out of college. There is no bank audit I cannot handle. Furthermore, as regards to your personal feelings for me. I am sorry, but I cannot accept them. I am a married woman. I am happy with my husband, and there is nothing you can say or do to change that, Daryl. So, if I have answered all your questions, I will be leaving. Good day, Mr. Dewight."

Daryl rolls his eyes, places his hands on his desk and leans forward. "Karla, I understand that you are not ready to be with me right now. So please have fun playing with your little boy toy for now. Karla, you and I both know love can get you only so far in life. I mean really now Karla, that boy cannot provide you with the basic needs a husband should." I shake my head at Daryl; he is so pathetic in his thinking. "Daryl, I know to you Derius lacks things in our marriage but let me make this one fucking thing clear to you.

THIS IS OUR MARRIAGE. I do not remember asking you to play our counselor. Yes, we have differences in age and even some forms of maturity, but we work through our issues together. The woman you thought you knew, is human. I have flaws, doubts, and even yes at times my own immature ways."

Daryl laughs as he leans back in his chair. "Immature is right! You fell in love with a baby! Risk time in prison for a child! You are seen as nothing more than a pedophile. Yet, still you claim this undying love for this boy; who can't even take care of you! I do not get your logic, Karla! That BOY is going to cost you a lot out of this world! What is so fucking special about him you would risk your freedom let alone the sheer embarrassment of just being with HIM?!" I can feel my anger boiling inside of me. I know that in the past I have had my doubts about my relationship with Derius. My own fears of how people viewed our union. Daryl maybe right in some ways. There are things at this time Derius is unable to provide me. BUT…

"You are right Daryl; there are things Derius may not be able to do right now. But there are some things he does better than YOU." Daryl sits straight up with a smirk on his face. "Enlighten me with those details please." I smile proudly at Daryl. "Derius is genuine; he holds back even when he is at the brink of a breakdown. Derius gives me all his attention, no matter what he has to do. He spoils me in ways only he can. Meaning I lack for nothing. I have all the joy and love any woman could have searched the world over. Lastly, Derius is MY HERO. He protects me from my own doubts and fears. As well as anyone else's, Derius is not intimidated by my success, he loves it! Derius is the head of our household because he knows his queen rules the house, while he rules our kingdom."

Daryl rubs his hands together and nods at me. I believe I have finally hit a nerve. "Karla. You may be right on some of the things, you say about him. I was not the most affectionate person when we were together…" *That reminded me I did have something to confront him about.* "OH YEA! About not being affectionate but you had time for Candice, right?!" Daryl's eyes widen as I mention Candice's name. "Karla, Candice is in the past. I am talking how I feel about you now."

Oh no, he was not going to moonwalk past this discussion. "Oh no Daryl, please tell me how you, the busy man, working for OUR benefit had time to sleep with Candice while we were dating." Daryl shakes his head at me, then stands up.

"Karla, you were not my dad's first choice for me to marry. He wanted me to marry Candice; he had always liked her. I have known Angela and Candice since middle school. So, when you and I would argue, she would always come be my shoulder to cry on. One night she was more than that. It only happened once, but I do regret that it did happen. She was distraught that I would not dump you for her, so she went and told people she was pregnant by me." I didn't have anything to say. *All of this crap was in the past right? Why do I even care*? "So, is that why you were engaged to her? Who was the other woman?" Daryl walks over to his office window and looks out.

"Angela must have told you. Yes, I have been engaged twice. Once to Candice, which would have never worked out because of my work hours. I could not stay home and babysit her all the damn time. Another woman named Karen, who passed away in the middle of our engagement." I stood up to get ready to leave. "Daryl I'm sorry for your loss, but I have to go. Take care of yourself." I walk towards the door, as I reach for the handle. Daryl spins me around and kisses me! The heat from his lips, shocks me as I freeze, lifeless in his arms. There was nothing there, not even my old college flame. I push Daryl off of me before I can yell at him, he pleads to me, "Karla, I am not the childish boy I was in college. I am a grown man! These feelings I have buried deep inside of myself for you are real and, will not go away. I love you, I always have! I know that back then I was too stupid and blind to hold on to you, but I am here now. No matter your situation, or status know that when the boy fails you… I am here."

***

I lean against the closed door that separates me from Daryl. *Karla you have a wonderful husband at home. You should go home to him.* I drive home to my house, to my husband, but I am filled with such guilt. Derius is my husband, I love him, and he is eighteen years old. My mind then wanders to Daryl, my first love, and first heartbreak. Now after all this time he wants to pledge and devote himself to me. Saying he will wait for me when Derius breaks my heart. Sorry, Daryl, my Hero will never do that. I know all my doubting him has broken his heart a few times, but not once has my Hero ever broken mine. That is why as I drive into my driveway, I can smile that I have everything I have ever wanted — everything Daryl now sees he should have given me in the first place. I go home to my husband. I walk inside the house to find Ayia playing on the floor, and I see a body lying next to her sound asleep, next to his textbook.

"I'm home." I watch him reach out for Ayia; she cuddles close to her daddy. Patting his head "There, There Daddy. Night Night." I watch Ayia kiss her Daddy on his forehead. She then gets up and walks off with her toy, into her room. I sit on the floor next to Derius. I rub his soft afro, letting my fingers swim in the undulating waves of his fresh shampooed hair and then I try to get off the floor. I am grabbed suddenly. Laughing as Derius opens his eyes to look at me. "Come lie down with me Mommy." I reposition myself on the floor with him, as he gives me his arm to rest my head on. Derius squeezes me in his arms, rubbing my belly. "How is my little man today? Mommy has been so busy; I hope you can forgive her. She is doing the best she can to provide for all of us until dad gets his coaching job."

I laugh squeezing his arm then leaning back so Derius can kiss me on my forehead. "You are home early today, Beautiful." I nod at him, kissing him on the cheek as he rests his head on my shoulder. "I missed my husband." Derius looks down at me raising an eyebrow. "Oh, you missed me huh? What type of missing are you talking about?" I roll my eyes at him, sometimes that is the only thing on his mind. Come to think of it; we haven't done anything since my birthday. So maybe he doesn't always have it on his mind. Derius rolls me onto my back, looking down at me. He stares at me for a while which starts to make me blush.

Derius smiles down at me. "Aww Beautiful, I love that I still can make you so bashful around me. I have not lost my charm at all." Leaning down his lips caress mine and I am instantly on fire. The heat that burns between us feels like a volcano has erupted. Our kiss deepens as I wrap my arms around Derius's neck. *This was the feeling I use to have with Daryl.* This childish, new type of love feeling that you have for the one you are in love with. Derius tightens his grip on my shoulders that sends waves through my body. His every touch confirms his love for me over and over again. We are suddenly interrupted by the sound of Derius yelling "Ouch, okay I'm sorry." We laugh as Derius gets off me "Little man is not playing with me, is he?" I shake my head as Derius helps me off the floor.

"Go take a nap Beautiful; dinner will be ready soon." I waddle upstairs to our bedroom. As soon as I hit the mattress, I am out cold. I wake up to the smell of food. Derius has placed my food on a tray with a rose, again. "He is such a romantic; I wonder if he learned that from his dad?" I eat my food and relax which I have not been able to do much due to all the drama and audit at work. I lie back thinking on things: *What in the hell did Daryl think when he kissed me? Why am I still thinking of this? Do I still have some feelings there for him because he was my first love? Karla stop obsessing over this and enjoy the fact you didn't waste your time on him.*

Before I know it I fall asleep again. The next thing I remember is the sun shining on my face waking me up. Ugh, I have that damn audit today and Derius's Championship basketball game tonight. I get up before anyone else and see a duffel bag packed for me. I look inside my jersey, jeans, and sneakers. Before I leave, I kiss Derius on the cheek, kiss Ayia, and tell my mom, who's already arrived, I will be home late. Once all of this is done, then I head out to the bank. When I get there, I get out of the car and walk toward the door. Angela meets me at the door. "So, what did that bastard want?" I shake my head as I can hear the rest of my employees coming up from behind. We all get right to work collecting the files and having them out for the auditors in the conference room we have prepared for them. We have set out the drinks and snacks for the auditors and then get ready for the bank to open.

Daryl walks in with coffee and donuts for the staff. He chats with the ladies up front for a while before coming into my office. I pretend not to see him standing in my doorway as he lightly taps the door. I do not even move my head as my eyes glaze up at him. "Are you ready for today Ms. Jacobs?" I roll my eyes and smirk at him "Yes Mr. Dewight, Mrs. Phillips is ready." Daryl sucks his teeth hearing my last name. He then closes the door to my office. "Karla, remember what I said the other day, okay?" I have no time to entertain this man any further. "Daryl, you had your chance to make me Mrs. Dewight, but you had other things that were more important to you, including Candice. I am now Mrs. Phillips; I would appreciate it if you would respect that and call me that from now on."

Daryl smiles at me then lean on my desk then stares at me a moment. *DAMNIT stop looking at me! No matter how I may feel about him right, does not excuse that fact that he is still fine as hell!* He stares at me for a moment before there is a knock at the door. He stands up straight, walks over to the door and opens it. Angela walks into my office staring at the both of us. *THANK YOU, GOD, SAVED BY THE BELL!* Angela looks over at me talking with her eyes, *Bitch what are you doing?* I look at her and laugh shaking my head. "Angela, what can I do for you?" Angela looks over at Daryl with a smug look. "The auditors have arrived and want to meet with you, Mrs. Phillips." I can barely hold in my laugh as she cuts her eyes at Daryl with a big smile on her face. Daryl's muscle in his face tightens, then relaxes as he walks out of the office.

"Girl you are a damn fool, you know, that right?" Angela laughs as she walks over to me. "Karla, do you think he is little mad or big mad." I get up laughing, then walk out to meet the auditors. Most of the day is questions, filing paperwork, and finding the paperwork. The day is speeding by when the time lunch comes. Daryl buys everyone food, and as I am eating my lunch in my office, he walks in. "How do you think we are doing so far?" I look up at him, nodding at me. "I think you did very well since we just opened. I am going to work on a spreadsheet that keeps track of the merger accounts. Because Sam, the head auditor, said that we should have a collective record as well as individual ones." I watch him sit down in front of me, looking around the office. As he looks around his eyes see the duffel bag.

Pointing at it he looks at me, "Karla, what is that?" I shake my head at him. "You think you have never seen a duffle bag before, Daryl." Daryl smirks then reaches over and grabs the bag. Before I could protest, he opens it. "Now what do we have here?" Daryl pulls out Derius's number jersey. "Aww, you have his jersey, which is so cute Karla. Do you bring him juice and snack for after the game too." I can feel the heat rising in my cheeks as I glare at him. Daryl laughs as he puts the jersey back in the bag and puts it back where he got it. "Derius has a Championship game tonight. Yes, I proudly wear my husband's jersey. As you already know I am a very supportive partner." Daryl nods his head as he folds his arms. "Championship game huh, you do know we have a dinner for the auditors tonight?" I remember the email, but I was going to miss that. "Yes, I know, but I have somewhere more important to be tonight, so I am going to have to miss it."

Daryl looks up at the clock then sighs. "It's a shame that you have to babysit him so much that you do not have time for adult activities." That statement makes me a little-pissed off. "That is because she is married. Married people have lives too Daryl." I look at Angela who is standing behind Daryl. Daryl laughs as he looks behind him and up at Angela. "Yes, but even adults should have some time to play. Don't you agree Angela?" Angela looks down as Daryl smirks, as she has a seat next to him. "Karla never was much for going out. She likes to be at home with her family. Get it, Daryl, Karla likes being with her husband and child." Daryl rubs his hands together then looks up at me. "Yeah, I know, she is a very compassionate, loving and understanding woman. Those are only just a few things I love about this woman."

Angela and I are speechless as Daryl gets up and leaves us. Once he is gone, I lie my head on the desk. "Karla, girl what in the hell?!" I shake my head on the cool desktop. After a few minutes, I look up Angela. "Why? Why now of all times does he want to have a heart? Why now does he love me so much?" Angela folds her hands in front of her. "Karla, girl, do not fall for that stupid man's foolishness. You have a HERO at home remember. We are going to support him today at his basketball game." I am nodding my head that she right when it hits me. "Excuse me, Ms. Green, did you say 'WE"?" Angela smiles, nods then winks at me. "Yes, we, Dexter invited me to the game too. So, I am going to support Derius." I smirk and give her that *whatever, but I know what you are up to* look.

Angela just shook her head as she walks out of my office. It has been a long day, and I am ready to go. I look up at the clock "Okay Karla; you have one more hour to go. Clear things with the auditors, get changed and head to Derius's game." I went online to look for the best route to take to the school. The less traffic I'm in, the better. Before I knew it was time to go. *THANK YOU, GOD!* Today has been one of the most strenuous days that I had in a while. I rub my stomach lightly. "Mommy is sorry for pushing you so hard honey." I get up and have a chat with the auditors; we did a pretty good job for our first run. Once they have left, I close out the accounts I am working on, log off, and go to get changed. Once I am dressed I check to make sure everything is closed and locked up.

My phone is ringing as I look at the caller ID I see that it's a text message from Angela. She has gone ahead to meet up with Dexter. As I head out the door, I see a man limping in front of his car. As I get closer, I see that it's Daryl. "Oh my god, Daryl, what happened to you?!" Daryl limps around to look at me. "Karla, I need your help. I twisted my ankle turning to save this little boy from walking into the street. I limped back to my car, only to see that I have locked my damn keys in it!" I sighed. Then helped him to my car. Once inside Daryl told me he had an extra key at his house. "So, do keep your house keys on your car ring?" Daryl shakes his head at me. "No, I do. However, I have an extra key hidden at my house in case of a situation like this." I look at the clock on my dashboard. "I'm sorry, Hero, I am going to be late."

I drive Daryl home, when we get there, Daryl has me go and look for the key. I search for about ten minutes. I walk back to the car, Daryl is on the phone. I look at the clock again on the dashboard. "DARYL!" Daryl raises a finger at me to be quiet. I roll my eyes at him, as my patience is wearing thin. Daryl sees the expression on my face, then points to the front of the house. I walk over toward the door again. He then points at a decorative box with his initials on it. I look at the box then touch it. It slides up, and there is the key. "THANK GOD FINALLY!" I take it out and unlock the door. I walk back out to get Daryl who is limping toward the door. I help him inside, leading him to the couch. Once he is sitting down, I close the front door. "Are you going to be okay?"

Daryl smiles up at me then motions towards the bar. "Karla, will you fix me a drink. I think after the day I have had I deserve it." I laugh at him as I go and fix him a glass of whiskey. I bring it to him; he takes it then looks over at me. "Are you not going to join me?" I reach in my pocket and pull out my cell phone. "I'm sorry Daryl, but Derius's game is almost over. I have to go." Daryl puts the glass on the coffee table then grabs my hand. "Please, Karla, have some real adult fun for once. I know you do not drink but have a drink with me." The thought of relaxing does sound inviting, especially in Daryl's manor. "Daryl, you forget one big thing, don't you?" Daryl looks puzzled for a moment then looks down at my stomach. "Come on Karla. I have known you almost forever. I know that you do not drink and that you are pregnant. I have some sparkling cider chilled on the bar just for you."

"Really? Well, I am running late, and I really should go. However, I am thirsty from looking for that damn key. So, I will have one glass and go." I walk back over to the bar, looking in the mini fridge and there are eight bottles of sparkling cider. As I took one out I see that it has my name on it. I open the fridge again and look at all the bottles. Yup, they all have my name on them. "Now why would he do that? I do not come to here like that." I shake my head, place the bottles back except one. I pour me a glass, then walk back to the couch and have a seat next to Daryl. "See now is that better. It sometimes pays to be an adult." I shake my head at him. "What makes you think that I am not an adult, Daryl?"

Daryl leans back, sips his whiskey and smiles at me. "I am only teasing you, Karla. I love the way you look when you get upset with me." I can do nothing but laugh at him. As I finish my drink, placing my glass on a coaster and stand up. "Well, I have to go now, by now the game is pretty much over, but I still have to be there." Daryl gets up from the couch and limps towards the door. When we are standing in the foyer, Daryl opens his arms for a hug. I walk into his embrace, his arms engulf me, and I inhale his scent. For a moment my heart skips a beat. I remember when I would have done anything to be in these arms. I squeeze him. Daryl strokes my hair lightly as I hear him sniffling. I try to break our embrace and look at him, but he squeezes me tighter.

"Don't look at me, Karla. Just let me have this moment for a little while. Just let me be a fool for a moment. Let me imagine that you are mine, once again." I cannot control my tears as I let him have his moment. Daryl did have feelings for me still. After everything he has been through and done. He still has the same feelings for me. Before I can say anything, Daryl let's go of me and opens the door for me. He turns his head away from me as I walk out the door. As I walk out the door, it closes behind me. I lean against the door frame. "Is he crying on the other side of this door?" The image of Daryl silently crying, makes me cry as I quickly walk back to my car and get in.

I drive off toward Derius's school. My mind going in a million different directions. I am thinking of Daryl and his pledge of love for me. Then I am thinking of Derius and our marriage. I am thinking of Ayia and this unborn child I am carrying. *Karla, you have to get yourself together. Too much stress is not good for the baby, remember.* I breathe in and out as I think of my blood pressure. The baby kicks me confirming that I do need to take it easy. Thinking of all the drama is bad for both of us. Soon I pull up to the school, and the parking lot is packed. I look around for a place to park. I finally find a place; then I waddle across the parking lot. I can hear the cheer of the crowd from outside. *I wonder who is winning, I know my Hero he is dominating this game.* As I walk across the parking lot, I hear a buzzer. Then the sound of the crowd roaring in celebration. *DAMNIT! I missed the game! Well at least I am here, Derius will want me here even if I missed it. Damn you, Daryl!*

As I get closer, I see people running and walking out back to their cars; by the looks of the students; I understand, Madison won the game! I get excited as I try to walk a little faster to meet Derius. It's taking me forever as I finally reach the stairs. I start up the stairs; it takes a little bit, but I make it eventually to the top. I look around for Derius, Franco or even Shatoya, but I do not see anyone. As I see players coming out, I ask if anyone has seen Derius. One of the guys looks around then points at a tree on the side of the building. "I think that is him over there; I can see his jacket from here." I can't see because of all the people, but I thank him. Then walk toward the tree on the side of the building. "Maybe he is waiting for me there?" As I keep walking people make room for me seeing that I am pregnant.

As I get closer, I can now see that it's Derius, because I can see his watch and jacket I bought him. I am all smiles until I notice that he is standing there with a female. She is light skin, with a black ponytail and is wearing a cheerleader's uniform. I watch closely; she is laughing and touching Derius. I raise an eyebrow at her gestures. *Little girl don't you know that he is*…. My thoughts are cut off because my mind, eyes, and heart can't believe what they are seeing. I watch as Derius leans down and kisses that girl! I watch as she wraps her arms around his neck and he grabs her tightly in his arms! My heart can't begin to explain to my brain or my eyes what is going on. Streams of tears fall outlining my cheeks as I watch them. I want to confront them, I want to yell out, but my mouth will not respond. All I can think of is that I had pushed him to this.

Karla, that breakdown Derius had was not just because of Daryl but because of you. You are the one who let Daryl in and let him meddle with your feelings for Derius. Now, look at the consequences of your actions. I cannot look anymore as I turn and quickly walking back to the car. After some effort, I finally make it back to my car. I get in and drive away, tires squealing. My mind is cloudy as my tears stream down my face. *NOT MY HERO! NOT DERIUS! HE WOULD NEVER DO THAT TO ME!?!* I can barely breathe as I speed down streets. I am not paying any attention to where I am or where I am going. I keep driving, screaming and praying this is all some terrible nightmare that I can wake up from. When I finally stop and look up, I am parked in front of Daryl's house.

CHAPTER SIX

THE INFRINGEMENT

"Yes! We won the game." I look around the stadium of the gym, but I do not hear or see Karla. The roar of the crowd is still ringing in my ears as the announcer calls me to the middle of the court. "Derius you have been selected as tonight's MVP, and you have the pleasure of cutting the net down." The announcer hands me the scissors. I jog over to the net, climb up the ladder and cut the net down. Then I swing it in the air as the crowd goes crazy. My teammates including Franco pick me up and placing me on their shoulders. This moment is one I will never forget. *Where is my Beautiful?* I smile for the cameras when my teammate put me down finally I speak to reporters. Once that is all clear, I look again for Karla. No sign of her anywhere. *Damn Beautiful did you miss the game?* Well, I did know that today was the audit at the bank.

I am still looking around for Karla when Franco walks over to me. "Yo, DK, what's the matter?" I shake my head as I still look for Karla. "I do not see my baby anywhere man! I wonder if she missed the game because of work?!" Franco pats my shoulder. "She might have DK, but she is probably waiting outside for you! It's crowded in here! With her being pregnant and all she might have felt safer outside!" I think he might be right, as I walk to the locker room to get showered and changed. Soon as I walk in, I feel the chill of a cooler of ice and water being dumped on me. "HOLY SHIT!!" Laughter echoes around me as everyone congratulates me on winning the game for them. I am freezing as I run to the shower hop in and turn on the hot water. Soon my body is relaxed again as I snatch off the wet clothes. I hear a knock at the door. "Uh, who is it?" Franco laughs as he opens the door slightly. "HEY MAN, I AM NAKED IN HERE! CLOSE THE DAMN DOOR!" I look at the door and see that Franco brought me my shower bag. "Oh, thank you, man." I hear Franco as he closes the door. "Next time I will let your ass stink." I hear him laugh then leave to get a shower.

Soon I am clean and fresh. I grab my stuff and walk over to my locker. I get dressed and check myself before reaching for my watch and jacket. "Hold up. Where is my jacket and watch?!" I start laughing because these fools are playing too much. "Alright now, I am ready to go to this party. So where is my jacket and my watch?" Everyone looks at me, shaking their heads. Concern soon hits me as I turn to look in my locker for my jacket and watch again. Panic sets in as I dump my duffle bag on the floor. No matter where I look they are not there! Franco walks over to me as I sit down on the bench with my hands on my head. "DK, man what is wrong?" I look up at Franco in total disbelief.

"Franco! Man, someone stole my watch and my jacket!" Franco looks in the locker, then in my duffel bag. "Are you sure man? I mean did you leave them in the car, maybe?" I rub the imprint that is on my wrist. "Franco. Look at my arm man. I barely take that damn watch off this wrist since Karla gave it to me. My jacket, I won't even wear the school jacket they gave me. I only wear my coach's jacket that Karla gave me our first Christmas. So, no, I didn't leave them in the car." Franco nods his head, patting my shoulder. "Yeah, you are right. You wear that watch and jacket everywhere! Come on man lets go and ask the guys at the party. Some left before the game was over maybe one of them have seen your watch and jacket." I attempt to calm down as I get up and leave with Franco. "Who in the hell would be stupid enough to steal my damn shit?!" I am still fuming mad as we walk out of the gym. Franco slaps me on the arm as he points at Shatoya. We walk over towards her as we get closer I notice she is holding something. "Derius, I found your jacket and watch!" I look at Shatoya with complete confusion. "Hold up where did you find them?"

Shatoya hands me my jacket and watch. "I came out to the car to get Franco's shirt, and I saw them on top of your car. I know that you would have never left it there." I am still confused as I put my jacket and watch on. "Man, maybe it was a joke, one of the guys pulled on you." Franco slaps me on his back, and I look at Shatoya. "Shatoya, have you seen Karla?" Shatoya shakes her head at me. Now I am getting worried. I grab my phone to call Karla. I listen to the phone ring twice.

When the phone finally picks up. "Beautiful, where are you? I am getting worried?" The next voice that comes across the line makes my blood boil. "She does not want to speak to you right now." I can't even think straight, as try to get my thoughts together. Franco grabs my shoulder, and I snatch away from him.

"Daryl. Put Karla on the phone!" Daryl sighs deeply on the phone. "Look, she is agitated right now. She does not want to see or speak to you right now. Can't you respect that?" The heat was rising from me as I listen to this bastard. "RESPECT! You of all people want to talk about RESPECT! What the FUCK do you know about respect huh Daryl!?! Did you RESPECT the fact that Karla is married? No, you have not shown one ounce of respect for our family, me or her! Don't you dare try to tell me about respecting MY WIFE. I live and breathe for her! Unlike you who abandoned her for your BULLSHIT EGO and A FALSE AMBITION! So, do not think of uttering a word about RESPECT when you do not know the FUCKING MEANING OF IT! NOW PUT KARLA ON THE PHONE NOW!"

I wait for an answer for a minute, then suddenly I hear the phone hang up! "HELLO! HELLO! DARYL! DARYL!" I scream as I pace the parking lot! "I am going to fuck that nigga up! You just wait, I am going to beat his ass!" Franco grabs me as I struggle to get out his arms. "DK! DK! Man calm down!" It takes a while struggling with him, but I do eventually calm down. Angela and Dexter come running over as I finally get myself together. "Derius! What is the matter?!" I am too upset even to try to explain. Franco tells them what happens. "WHAT?! I am going to call her right now!" I watch Angela call Karla, but she only gets the voicemail. "Her phone is off! What in the hell is going on here?!"

I shake my head as I sit on my car. "I have no idea, Angela. I called her a few minutes ago and do you know who answered her phone?" Angela shakes her head at me, then raises an eyebrow. "Who?!" My temperature is rising again as I roll my eyes. "Daryl." Angela's expression is priceless; she is frozen for a few minutes. "OH NO HELL! DARYL?! HOLD THE FUCK UP!" I watch Angela dial a number than when they answer she goes in. "HELLO?! WHO IN THE

FUCK DO YOU THINK YOU ARE?! WHERE IN THE HELL IS KARLA?!" I jump up to run over to get a good listen. "Angela calm down. It's not like that. Karla just wanted some space from that boy she takes care of. I assure you that she is safe, she is lying down on the couch right now." Franco grabs me before I can snatch the phone from Angela. Pulling me back to speak to me. "DK! No man, that nigga is not worth it. Just let him talk to her, then you will get your answers when she is finished."

I stand back from Angela as she goes on. "Uh huh, so why is Karla's phone off?" She listens to Daryl tell her the situation. "WHO ARE YOU TO CUT IT OFF?! SHE IS MARRIED TO HIM DARYL, AND HER HUSBAND IS WORRIED ABOUT HER!" I can do nothing more than pace in front of my car as Franco tries to keep me as calm as he can. Finally, Angela gets off the phone then walk over to me pointing at me. "Derius, I have no idea what has happened, but YOU BETTER FIX IT!" I put my hands up in defense as I shake my head and shrug my shoulders. "Angela, I promise I have no idea what is going on?! All I did was call her, and he answered telling me that she didn't want to talk to me. Now, what did that ASSHOLE have to say?"

Angela looks at me then sighs. "He said that she came speeding up his driveway. He saw her out of his window, he limped out there and got her out of the car. He thought she might be hurt because of the baby. Karla was crying so much she couldn't even speak. So, he had her lie down on the couch. Karla fell asleep in her own tears. Then you called looking for her. He assumed that you were the problem, so Daryl told you that she didn't want to talk to you." This is making no sense at all! "Why did she go to him?! Of all the fucking people in the world Karla why did you have to go to his ass?!" Angela punches me in the stomach to get my attention. "YOU HAVE TO GO GET YOUR WIFE! Karla is weak right now, and you know how she gets when she is weak. Besides I like you better than Daryl."

I smile at the compliment. I nod then look at her. "I have no idea where he lives!" Angela smiles then give me the directions to his house. I look behind me Shatoya points in the direction of my car. I look, and Franco is standing there with the passenger door open. "LET'S GO GET MRS. PHILLIPS" I run over, get inside the car and speed off. I am boiling mad as I drive to Daryl's house. "I'm gonna whoop his ass! Just wait I am going to fuck his whole world up!" Franco screams at me to stop the car. I pull over as Franco hops out. "NIGGA! Get out of the car, let me drive! You are too hyped up over this, and you are not getting me killed!" With that, we switch sides, but that does not stop me from being pissed off! "DK, we whooping asses now! We are fucking that niggas world up! DK stay calm, we are going to find out what is going on soon."

I am trying to stay calm as we reach Daryl's house. I see Karla's car parked in front of his house. I get so pissed off that I jump out the car and head straight for the door. Beating on it screaming "KARLA!" I scream out a few more times before the door opens and I see Daryl staring at me in his robe! He walks out of the house closing the door behind him. "Look! This is a residential neighborhood, not a damn playground. What are you doing here?!" I step up to his face, then stare him right in the eyes. "I am here; get my WIFE!

Now, where is Karla?" Daryl shakes his head as he smiles at me. "You don't listen do you boy… I grab him by the robe. I do not have time for this shit! I want to know why in the hell is Karla here! "Daryl quit fucking playing with me. Where is my wife?!" Daryl yanks out of my grasp as Franco grabs me from behind.

"Stop being a child! She does not want to see you at the moment! I am sure when she wants to talk to you she will. For right now the best thing you can do is to leave her alone." I struggle to get out of Franco's arms when I see the door open up behind Daryl. Karla walks out and stares at me a minute. "Karla, baby…." "Save it DERIUS!" Karla marches over to me and looks me over. "Karla, baby are you okay? What is wrong?" She looks up at me with tears building in her eyes. I look over at Daryl, who folds his arms in front of him and gives me a smirk. I look back at Karla as I am about to say something she slaps me across the face. "I HATE YOU DERIUS! I DO NOT WANT TO SEE OR TALK TO YOU RIGHT NOW!" I stand there stunned not because my face is throbbing but because I have no idea what the hell is going on!

I attempt again to reach out to speak to Karla, but she is not having it as she walks away from me. I walk over to her grabbing her from behind. I hold her and lean down. "Beautiful, I have no idea what is going on, but please talk to me... Karla struggles in my arms then finally pushes me away from her. She turns around glaring at me with tears in her eyes. "DO NOT TOUCH ME. GO AWAY DERIUS!" She walks back toward the door, looks back at me crying, and then walks back inside. There is nothing I can do but watch her walk away. Franco walks over to me. "Man, what is wrong with Karla?!" I shake my head, and I have no idea what is going on here. I look over at Daryl who is still standing there with his arms folded.

I walk over to him, I do not want to ask him this, but right now this is important. At least until I can figure out what is going on with Karla. "Daryl, keep an eye on her for me. I have no idea what is going on, but I am going to leave her alone for now." Daryl nods then walks back to the door. Before going in Daryl looks back at me. "Hey! I do not know what is going on with you two, but if you do not fix it soon. You will lose her to ME!" I glare at him as I watch him walk back inside and close the door. My mind is completely blank as I walk back the car and get in on the passenger side. Franco gets in the car, starts it and as we pull off, I can't keep my eyes off of the door. "What in the hell just happened Franco?"

Franco looks over at me shrugs, then sighs at me. "I wish I knew DK. Whatever it is though you better fix it. She looked like she was going to break at any moment. I heard what that nigga said to you. If she loses faith in you again, you may lose her FOR REAL this time." The reality of his words stung me like sharp needles. Karla did look like she was finished this time. Our whole relationship has been this challenge, a test to see if we can keep it together. More times than most I believed we were winning against the odds. With the shit, my mom pulled, our separation, and now this. How am I supposed to keep fighting to be the good man, when she keeps pushing me away? My Beautiful is a fragile woman. She is so scared that her happily ever after will turn out to be an illusion. Thinking about myself, maybe I have had that same fear that our paths crossing was just a dream that I could never wake up from.

My thoughts are interrupted by Franco parking the car in front of his apartment. "Hey DK, are you going to be okay?" I look over at him nodding. Suddenly I hear his phone ring. He shakes his head, then looks down at the phone. "OH, SHIT! IT'S COACH!" I lean my head back on the headrest. Dealing with all of this, I completely forgot about the championship party; not to mention my damn awards. I look at Franco giving him the cut off sign. Franco nods as he talks to the coach, telling me that Karla was not doing well, so I took her home. Once he got off the phone, he yawns then looks at me. "You should go home and get some sleep. Talk to her tomorrow. Make Karla talk to you tomorrow."

We switch places as I go to get in the driver's seat. Franco hugs me; I slap him on the back of the head. "I will talk to Karla tomorrow. Check on Shatoya. I am fine; I will be okay to drive home." Franco checks if I will be okay one more time and after a half smile finally goes inside. I head home, I do not want to, but I know Momma Ellie is probably worried to death by now. As I drive, I try not to replay the events of tonight in my head. Tonight was supposed to be a great night too. My team won the championship, I was picked as the M.V.P, and everyone was supposed to be at the celebration party. I rub the back of my head, then shake it. It did not go that way at all. *Yup, I ended up upset, worried and perplexed. I couldn't find my shit when I finish showering, I couldn't get my wife on the phone when I was looking for her, and in the end, I couldn't understand why my wife is mad at me or at that bastard's house!*

I finally make it home. I am exhausted physically and mentally. I want to go to bed now. I want to wake up and this to having been a bad dream. I walk into the house; it's quiet…too quiet. I call out to Momma Ellie with no response. I begin to panic as I rush through the house looking for Momma Ellie and Ayia. After screaming my head off, no one is home. I walk into the kitchen and see a note on the fridge. I sigh as it's from Momma Ellie: "Derius, I got a call from Karla telling me to take Ayia to my house. What, happened son? Whatever it is I know that you will get the both of YOU through it. Love Momma." I turn around, leaning my back on the fridge. "At least you believe I can Momma Ellie. Right now, I am not so sure."

All I can do after reading that is go to bed or better yet try to. Once I got in the bed, I realized sleep was far from my mind. I just kept looking at Karla's side of the bed. Since we have married, I have just gotten used to seeing her snoring next to me. I think about all the times; I would wake up to it and smile. Cuddle up to her rubbing her belly and talking to our son. Those are the moments I want right now. Not this bitter uncertainty of not knowing if I will be losing Karla once again having this time alone. I try to think of what in the hell happened tonight. Nothing is clear, and I am growing more and more frustrated just thinking about this shit! *Karla slapped me? The only thing is why did she slap me? What did I do that pissed her off so much?*

Anger, frustration, and exhaustion get the best of me finally as I pass out. It's not a peaceful sleep I can tell you that. As nightmares plague, my dreams and I toss and turn. I am awakened suddenly by drawers being shut violently. I jump up and see Karla packing a suitcase! I am half out of it as I shake my head clear and look. "BABY! What are you doing?!" Karla doesn't even look at me as she packs her clothes into the suitcase. I jump out of bed standing in front of the suitcase and grabbing her shoulders. Karla snatches away from me. "DO NOT TOUCH ME! I am going to stay with my mom and dad for a few days." I am at a loss for words as anger takes over and I place my hand over the suitcase she is packing. "TALK TO ME! What in the hell is going on here?!"

Karla looks up at me then shakes her head. "I can't trust you right now Derius. I need time to figure out what to do." I sigh deeply "What do you mean you can't trust me? What have I done to deserve any of this?! What is this because I came to Daryl's house last night?" Karla looks at me then points "No that is NOT it! You know why I am pissed off! Stop standing there playing like you're the fucking victim here! What did you do last night!?!" I was baffled. "I came to see how you were doing… "BEFORE THAT! WHAT DID YOU DO?!" I thought about it a moment. "I won the game; I went to take a shower…. Karla slaps me again. This time I grab her shoulders! "WHAT THE FUCK IS THAT FOR?! What in the hell happen that you THINK you can't trust me anymore! Stop going around in the circles and tell me directly!"

Karla snatches out of arms, marches over to my jacket and throws it at me. I catch it when I feel a stinging sensation as I look down at my watch on the ground. Karla points at it, my watch on the floor. "I saw you. God knows I didn't want to believe it at first, but that damn watch kept glistening in the light. I couldn't think straight. I wanted to run up to you and smack the shit out of you!" Karla stops right there, waving her arms at me as she continues to pack. I let Karla's words sink in as I think them over. "She saw me in my watch? When?" I turn to Karla leaning on the bed. "Beautiful…" She cuts me a sharp stare. "Don't call me that." I sigh as I keep myself calm. "Fine. Karla. What did you mean that you saw me? I looked for you with Franco when I got out of the shower."

Karla stops packing and stares at me. "Oh, you did, is that when you ran into the bitch, I saw you with?!" I am taken back from her response. "Hold on, what bitch?! What are you talking about Karla?" Karla leans over and rubbing her eyes. "Are you okay?" She waves me off and shakes her head. "Don't concern yourself with me now Derius! You were not concerned about Ayia or me when you did what you did." Still leaning on the bed. "Karla, I do not know what you are talking about? What have I done?" Karla is finally finished packing her things. "It doesn't matter now. Play dumb all you want to Derius. But I saw you in your jacket and watch with that bitch under that tree. I hope she was worth you losing your wife and children for!" I blink as I realize that Karla thinks I cheated on her! "Hold on Karla!" I step in front of her, and she tries to shove me out the way.

"You said you saw me in my jacket and watch right?" She looks up at me with tears building in her eyes before I can say anything else. I see Angela walk in and push me out the way. "Let's go, Karla. You don't have to keep making her relive it, Derius. How cruel are you going to be?!" I am shocked as I let her walk out of the room, but I follow them. As I walk them to the door, I think over what she has just said. It makes no sense to me. I didn't cheat on Karla. I close the door behind them as they get in the car. It hits me again what I was about to say. I run out to the car, banging on the car window. Karla looks at me, then rolls down the window. "Karla! You said you saw me in my jacket and watch. But when I got done with the game, I couldn't find my jacket or my watch in my locker! Baby, it wasn't me you saw I SWEAR!"

Karla looks at me then starts to cry. She reaches for my hand, but Angela pulls it back. "I saw you Derius, and you were wearing your jacket and watch!" Karla looks at me then shakes her head at me. "When I saw you at Daryl's you had them both on too. " I attempt to explain, but Angela backs up and drives off. Leaving me standing in the driveway at a complete loss. I go back into the house, slamming the door. Screaming at the top of my lungs; I run upstairs as I hear my phone ring. I am hoping it Karla to let me finish explaining, but it's Franco. I do not want to talk to anyone right now. I am still confused at what has happened. *She said she saw me in my jacket and watch. There is no way she could have seen me. I couldn't even find my jacket or watch when I got out of the shower.*

At that moment I didn't want to think about that. I sit on the bed and replay Karla leaving in tears. The only thing I could think of is….

Did I just lose my wife? I pick up the phone and call her several times. Angela hung up on me, yells at me to stop calling, but I can't stop, till finally, when I call the phone is completely turned off. Franco calls me several times too, but I am too depressed to hear it. I call off work and stay in the house. I do not take any phone calls from anyone and don't bother listening to my voicemails. I fall deeper into depression as I listen to sad songs play. I cry a few times, I curse in anger and finally drop from my own defeat. None of this shit matters if there is no resolution. The whole weekend is like a blur to me as I wake on Monday morning.

The phone is ringing once again. I look over to see it, Franco, again. I answer this time. "Hey, DK, man you do know we have a test, today right?! Where in the hell are you?!" I totally forgot I have school today! I look at the clock on my phone. *OH SHIT!* It will take me at least thirty minutes to get to school! I rush to throw some clothes on and grab my bag. I speed all the way to school, lucky for me there are no cops around. I make it to class with ten minutes to spare. Franco and I are in the same class. He looks at me like

"Nigga are you crazy?!" I shake my head as I sit next to him. For the rest of the day, I take all my mid-term tests, it's the week before Spring break. Once classes are over Franco and I are walking towards our cars. "Man, why did you not answer your phone at all this weekend?" I shake my head at my brother; Franco is really concerned about me.

"Look, man, I didn't want to talk to anyone. I even called off work both days. I just needed to chill out you know. Karla left and went to her parents' house for a while; she took Ayia too. Franco, she said she saw me cheating on her. She said something about seeing my jacket and watch, but you remember when we came out the game I couldn't find them." Franco thinks a minute as he is thinking I see Phillip. He walks over to us and gives me a pound. Franco points at Phillip. "You! Phil, did you see Derius's girl on Friday night?" Philip shakes his head before I can say anything else. He looks at my jacket. "Johnisha just bought one of those jackets for her brother." I am curious now, so I raise my arm to show off my watch. "Oh, snap you got the same watch she got her brother too!"

Franco and I both look at each other. "Oh, really man. Yeah, my wife gave me mine a while back. When did Johnisha show you the gifts for her brother?" Phillip smirks then rubs his hands together. "She wanted me to try them on Friday night. You remember I twisted my ankle so I couldn't play that night. Doctor's orders, so I just came to the game. Johnisha met me outside by that tree right outside the gym, and she had me try on the stuff. Then she kissed me; we kissed for a minute too. She told me that she kissed me as a thank you for making sure the jacket and watch would fit her brother." My blood was boiling at this point. Johnisha had set my ass up! Quite well I might add because Karla thought it was me! "Thank you, Philip. I have all I need. By the way, have you seen Johnisha around here today?"

Phillip nods then point toward the football field. "I saw her on the field for practice. I thank him again, then turn to Franco who is already walking in the direction of the field! "YO! Franco wait up!" I catch up him, and he is turning red. "That Bitch, MAN! Johnisha did that bullshit on purpose, and I am about to straighten her ass out!" I grab my brother's arm. "Hold up Franco! We are going go to do this together. I have a few choice words that I want to say to her, as well, my brother." We both run towards the football field. We arrive in minutes, and sure fucking enough Johnisha is there practicing. She looks up, sees me and smiles. I wave her over to us. She runs towards us with her at least DD cups bouncing towards us. Both Franco and I are in a trance for like a minute tops.

Before we can think straight again, she is standing in front of us. "Hey, Derius." I begin to smile, but then I remember why the hell I am there! "COME WITH ME!" I pick her up and throwing her over my shoulder. She squeals in excitement. I carry her to the tree in front of the gym. I put her down then I lean over her. "Now that I have you here. Let's reenact that little scene you played out for my wife Friday night shall we." Johnisha leans against the tree, looks up at me and smiles. "It was just a joke Derius. You don't gotta be so damn sensitive 'bout it" I begin to laugh, then Franco starts laughing soon we are all laughing. Suddenly I look down at her still laughing. "Do you think my wife found your joke funny, huh?" Johnisha shakes her head as she keeps laughing when she looks back at my face. I have an icy look in my eyes.

"Okay…Okay. I had one of the guys get your jacket and watch out of the locker. I had Philip to pretend to be you, and yes, I set Karla up to catch you. You ignored me! I have never had any guy ever to ignore me before. You wanted nothing to do with me. I thought if I got rid of her, then I could finally have a chance with you. I like you Derius. I'm sorry." I shake my head at this stupid bitch! "You're sorry! You are sorry! You are a sorry excuse of the female species! What in the hell would EVER make you think I would like you?! You are as fake and stupid as they come. You ruined MY LIFE so YOU could get a chance to DATE ME! ARE YOU REALLY FUCKING SERIOUS?!" Franco pushes me back from her because I do not hit women ever, but this bitch needs to be slapped!

Franco looks at Johnisha shaking his head. "Do you want to know why Derius will never date you yet alone look at you from now on out? Johnisha looks at me with tears in her eyes. "Why?" Franco laughs as he wipes his face. "Because you are nothing more than a pathetic, spoiled brat! You think of NO ONE but yourself and what you can get others to do for you. Look how you played our boy, Philip. You are a virus that needs to be vaccinated. All women like you need your asses whipped. You are the main reason men look down upon good women. You are a disease that has infested this school for far too long. Derius has no respect for a worthless, immature, selfish child like you! Now or Ever! Never approach my boy again for any reason, or I will make sure that two of Florida's finest will beat your ass for sure. Can you fight, Johnisha?"

Johnisha shakes her head as tears stream down her reddened cheeks. "Then you will not take my words lightly, will you?! Now get the hell out of here!" Johnisha looks at me. I look at her with disgust and shake my head. "I'm sorry Derius." We watch as she runs away crying. I look at Franco then slap him on the back of the head. "Two of Florida's finest, and whom would that have been Franco?!" Franco looks at me shaking his head, shrugs his shoulders. "Who else would have come up here and beat her ass for you with no hesitation huh? I can only think of two names Keisha and Shantell." All I could do is laugh because that was so true. Even after everything that happens between us, they would have come up here and beat her ass for me.

I felt better since I had finally found out who had caused all this bullshit between Karla and me. I replay the event in my mind as if I were looking at from Karla's eyes. "Oh, Franco man. I can see why she was so hurt. Just the mere thought of me confronting her about Daryl then to see that sent her over the edge." Franco agrees with me. "Philip does look like you from a distance." Dexter and Robby come walking out of the gym together. Dexter walks up to me. "Man, because you are fucking up with Karla, Angela doesn't want to date me anymore!" I raise my hands in defense. "I just found out the truth about Friday, Dex." I then go on to explain what Johnisha had done. Dexter is so mad he could spit fire. "ARE YOU KIDDING ME?! SHE DID ALL THAT SO YOU WOULD GIVE HER A SHOT!"

Robby then looks at me, then sighs deeply. "Look Derius, I have to apologize to you too man. I am the one who took your jacket and watch that night. Johnisha told me that the guys were going to play a prank on you because you won the M. V.P. So, I got the stuff for her. Yo, I swear I didn't know what she was really going to do with it, man." I nodded then told him it was cool. I got my stuff back, and now I can clear things up with my wife… My phone rings and I see its Karla's cell phone. I walk away for a minute. "Baby I am so happy you called me…" I am interrupted by Shatoya crying on the phone. "Shatoya?!" Franco hears Shatoya's name and runs over. "Man, what is it DK!?! Man, tell me that she is okay?! I listen for a minute then drop the phone. I am in dazed as the words echo in the mind. "Karla fainted and is now at the hospital."

Franco shakes me out of my trance, but by the look on his face, I wish I hadn't. "DK! Man snap out of it we gotta go!" We run to my car, and Franco is driving again because I can't even think, let alone drive. We reach the hospital in a matter of what feels like seconds. I jump out, run inside and almost kill myself as I hit the counter. "PLEASE! I AM LOOKING FOR MY WIFE! HER NAME IS KARLA PHILLIPS! THEY BROUGHT HER IN BECAUSE SHE FAINTED!" It took the nurse a few minutes to calm me down but once Franco, and she did. She told me she was in the emergency room. When we reach the emergency room area, I see Momma Ellie. She runs over to me, crying in my arms. I look at Robby J who is shaking his head. Franco hugs Shatoya who is crying her heart out.

My reactions are from pure shock; I can't even cry right now. "Can someone tell me what is going on?" Before anyone can say anything, I see the doctor come out. I try to get his attention but notice he walks over to a man who had just run in with Angela. I feel like I am walking in slow motion toward them. I hear the doctor say "She is not doing well, we are trying to get her blood pressure down right now. But if we can't, we might have to look into other options. Rest assured your wife will be just fine." I stop in my tracks as I watch the doctor and DARYL talk about MY WIFE! Soon the doctor walks away from him. I grip my fist against my side. The level of anger that is building in me explodes. I run over to Daryl punching him in the face.

We start fighting, and everyone is trying to break us up. "THIS SHIT IS ALL YOUR FAULT! ALL THE STRESS YOU PUT HER THROUGH WITH YOUR BULLSHIT!" Daryl swings at me again, hitting me in the side. "ME! IF YOU WOULD HAVE STAYED IN A CHILD'S PLACE, SHE WOULD NOT BE HERE!" Franco and Robby J grab me dragging me back. I snatch out of their arms, running over slamming Daryl into the wall and punching him in the face again. "I AM HER FUCKING HUSBAND, NOT YOU DARYL! GET THE FUCK OVER IT!" Daryl holds the side of his face as he stands up. Wipes the blood from his nose and sniffs. "Enjoy that little title for now, because your days of playing house with Karla are almost over."

Before I can hit his punk ass again, Robby J grabs me with both hands. "NO SON! He is not worth it! Daryl gets the hell out of here; Karla's family is with her now!" Daryl nods and walks off staring me up and down. Robby J walks me outside to get some air. "Derius, son, this is not the time to be fighting that fool!" I agree this is not the time to be doing that shit. "I'm sorry Robby J, but you know how much patience I have had with that nigga! When I saw the doctor talking to him like he was her husband I just snapped. I'm sorry that you saw me like that." Robby J pats me on the back. "I understand son but know that Daryl can have his pipe dreams all he wants. I have already met the man who is right for my daughter. You Derius, you complete her world, no matter who thinks it's not you, it's YOU. I liked Daryl at one time; he was an okay guy. Anyone can be liked. I respect you Derius, and that is not an easy thing to get from me, you hear me. Respect is always earned and never given son."

Those words are the same words if my dad had been there he would have given me. Robby J gives me a big hug; it's a moment that I will never forget. We go back inside. The doctor walks over to Robby J and asks where Karla's husband went. Robby J slaps me on the back and walks off. The doctor is confused as I explain that I am Karla's husband. The doctor then describes the situation at hand. "Mr. Phillips your wife is suffering from preeclampsia, a condition that is associated with the high blood pressure she had when she was brought in. We have been trying for a while to get her blood pressure down. But Mrs. Phillips developed seizures during the process. Your wife now has eclampsia. This is where the news can get bad Mr. Phillips. Eclampsia is a life-threatening complication. Because the preeclampsia was not treated in time, Mrs. Phillips and the baby are in real danger."

"What are you saying, doctor?!" I can hardly keep it together as the doctor nods and tells me again what is going on with Karla. "I am saying that we have two choices in this matter, Mr. Phillips. We have to deliver the baby now or terminate the pregnancy altogether. We can't allow the pregnancy to continue. Right now, our only option is an emergency C-section. We do not have much time either, Mr. Phillips. Karla and the baby's blood pressures are too high. If we continue to try to control it and not make a decision you could lose them both." I grab the doctor by his lab coat. "Doctor, if we do this will they both be okay?" Tears are streaming down my face; I can't control myself from shaking. The thought of losing Karla and the baby are tearing me apart. The doctor looks at me with concern in his eyes. "Mr. Phillips, I will do my very best, I promise you. Mrs. Phillips blood pressure is just not coming down. This is the only option we have, but the complication is that you could lose one of them, or the child could be born prematurely. Now being born prematurely is not bad as long as the vital functions are fine." I nod, closing my eyes — all I can see Karla's face the very last time I saw her. She didn't look well at all. I remember asking her was she okay. She just shrugged it off. I open my eyes, looking at the doctor. I had a tough decision to make here. Save my wife or my child. How could God do this to me? How could I ever choose to save one or the other?

I wipe the tears from my face. Look at the doctor and make my decision. "Doc, save my family. Do the C-section, save my wife and my baby." The doctor nods and runs off. I watch him leave; then I get a phone call. At this time, I do not want to talk to anyone, but it's Karla's doctor, Mr. Gray. "Hello, Mr. Phillips. I just got the message from Doctor Roma. I am so sorry I am not there. I had a death in the family, and I am in California at the moment.

"Nonetheless, Doctor Roma is a fantastic substitute. He will do his ultimate best to come out with the best results possible. Karla had missed her last few appointments with me. I had warned her a month or so ago about stress not being suitable for herself or the baby." I listen to Dr. Gray then hang up.

I am emotionally drained as I look over at my family. They all have hopeful looks on their faces. How do I walk over there and tell them the news that I have just received. I walk over to everyone. They huddle around me as I tell them what the doctor just told me. I grab Momma Ellie's hands first. She would need the most support. "Well, the doctor is going to have to do an emergency C-section on Karla." Momma Ellie's reaction is not one I want to see. Momma Ellie squeezes my hand. "So, what does that mean Derius? What is wrong with my baby?!" I grab her close and hug her tightly. I can't look into her eyes as tears build in mine. "Momma, don't you worry they are going to do their best to keep them both with us." Momma Ellie pushes me back from her, grabbing at my shirt. "WHAT?! WHAT DO YOU MEAN HE IS

GOING TO TRY TO KEEP THEM BOTH WITH US?! DERIUS, PLEASE TELL ME!"

I cry as I shake my head. I explain clearly about everything, but I do not get it all out when they wheel Karla out fast! I panic as I run over to the stretcher. "KARLA! BEAUTIFUL, I AM HERE! STAY WITH ME KARLA!" The nurses rush her off; the doctors stop quickly. "We have to do it now, Mr. Phillips! We are moving her to the O.R. to do the C-section! Follow me please!" We all run with the Doctor to the operation waiting room. He looks at me and assures me again he will do all he can. Then he runs inside to get ready for surgery. Momma Ellie is a wreck as she cries in Robby J's arms. I get on the phone and call Karla's sisters and Anthony. Anthony screams through the phone. "DERIUS! What is going on?! Where is my baby sister, man?!" When I finally get him calm telling him I will contact him as soon I know something.

Once I have time even to think straight, I try to keep Ayia calm. She is upset because everyone is crying. I rock her to sleep in my arms. I look around at everyone. Franco and Shatoya bring us all food from the cafeteria as we wait for the news. This has to be longest day of my life. My mom calls many times for updates. I tell her that I am holding up and I will call her. As I sit there with my mind completely blank. Angela walks over to me. "I know you do not want to, but he loves her too Derius. Be the bigger man and call him, will you?" I give Ayia to Momma Ellie and walk outside with Franco. "Do you think I can be the bigger man right now, Franco?" Franco nods at me then motion at me to do it. "You have always been the bigger man DK. That is one of the many reasons Karla loves you so much. She knows no matter what you will ALWAYS do the right thing."

I take a deep breath and then dial. Daryl's voice comes over raspy and broken. "Please tell me that she is safe. All I want to hear right now is that Karla is still alive." Part of me wants to be mad because he didn't ask about the baby, but that is all he is concerned about. "Right now, I am waiting to see if she is going be. I had them do an emergency C-section to try to save her…" "WHAT?! See this is why you are just a child. You are supposed to save Karla! Nothing else matters besides that!" I breathe in deeply as I am about to snap, but

I'm not. "Daryl. That nothing you are referring to is my life. Both of them matter very much to everyone that is in Karla's life including her. So, for you to only be concerned about my wife's well-being and not our child's confirms your selfishness. I am telling you that she is in surgery only because I thought you were a true friend of hers. I see now that this call like everything else about you is full of your ego, selfishness, and narcissistic attitude. You do not see Karla as a woman who loves her life or children, but a trophy. A tangible item you have yet to claim. My wife is not a prize, Daryl, and my unborn child is not an obstruction." Daryl says nothing else hangs up the phone.

Franco looks at me shaking his head. "Did he just…" I cut him off with a sigh, "Do not even bother with it, Franco. I did what I was asked and that it is all I am doing for that nigga. Let's go back inside." We walk back into the waiting area and see the doctor walking out. I run over to him, but the expression on his face does not look hopeful. "Mr. Phillips. We were fortunate to get the baby out in time. The internal bleeding had begun, and we had to work fast to get the baby out." I pat the doctor on the back. "Oh, thank you, god! You did well doctor. So that means that the baby and Karla are doing okay right?" The doctor ran his hands through his hair. "Mr. Phillips, with Mrs. Phillips blood pressure being so high and then getting the baby out. She lost a lot of blood; we had to place her into an induced coma."

All I could do is look at him with a blank stare. The doctor pats me on the back, then gave me a hopeful smile. "Mr. Phillips. Do not be discouraged, putting Mrs. Phillips in a coma will help her heal. This way she will get the blood transfusion she needs, and we can monitor the blood pressure. She will be okay if her body and mind are calm." I understand what the doctor was saying, but my heart would not let it sink in. The thought of Karla in a deep sleep, unable to talk to me, to see our son or let me explain to her heart that I was never unfaithful to her. It was tearing me apart inside. There was nothing I could do at that moment but sigh deeply. "She will be alright, right doctor?" The doctor nodded confidently with his hand on my shoulder. As long as he was sure that Karla would wake up to me, I felt better. Now it was time to break the news to the family.

"Mr. Phillips…" I cut him off telling him to call me Derius. He smiled then tells me that they will be moving Karla into a private room in a little while; he will come to get us when they were finished. Soon after the doctor left I walk over to Momma Ellie and grab her hands as everyone gathers to hear news on Karla. I then tell them everything the doctor just told me. Momma Ellie almost faints, Angela breaks down crying, and Shatoya keeps saying "What, Why? That's not fair." I try to assure them that the doctor said that she would be fine after a few days of monitoring. I inform them that this was the best action to ensure Karla and baby are safe. A few minutes of crying and hugging calms everyone down a little bit. Momma Ellie calls Anthony and Karla's sisters telling them they need to come to Georgia.

***

Everyone seems calm enough until we see Karla in her hospital bed. I try to stand strong, but it's Ayia who breaks us all. She runs over to the bed, smiling and tugging at

Karla. When there is no response, she looks at me. "Daddy, why is Mommy still sleeping?" How do I explain to our daughter that her mom is still fighting for her life? I can't, as I kneel and gather Ayia in my arms trying not to cry. My tears make it hard to swallow. Nothing helps, as I look up to see Momma Ellie nearly about to break down herself. The doctor walks over to me then kneels to Ayia. She looks at him with a smile. "Your mommy is exhausted. She just had your baby brother, and she needs to sleep for now. Is it alright for her to sleep for now?" Ayia smiles, nodding. "Mommy needs to sleep now?" I nod too as I hug her I look over at the doctor mouthing "THANK YOU!" He pats me on the back, then gets up and walks over to Momma Ellie.

"Karla's vitals look very good. She will be out for a few days, and we are monitoring her, but all looks very good. So, for now, please do not worry and enjoy your grandson. His major functions are almost perfect. I think they may have had his delivery date a little off." Momma Ellie smiles and hugs the doctor. "Thank you, doctor, that is exactly what we will do. I so appreciate everything you are doing for my daughter." The doctor walks away. When we sit in the room, all we hear is beeping of the machines, and the monitors. I see IVs attached to Karla. I can barely keep my composure as I stare at my wife. Momma Ellie pulls a chair up next to Karla and holds her hand. I am almost frozen in place with Ayia in my arms. It's her hugging me that brings me back to this reality.

Franco and Shatoya look at me. All I can do is shake my head in disbelief. Even though I feel so detached from Karla right now. She still looks so beautiful. We all sit in the room as Robby J says a prayer for each of us. I then take Ayia to see her little brother. Because he had to be born a few months early the doctor has him in the infant ICU. They are monitoring his heart rate, making sure his body functions are working correctly. But not by the look of his cute chubby body, and alert eyes. I smile and laugh as Ayia waves hi to her little brother. The nurse then walks over to me asking me. "So, what is this little one's name?" Karla and I had thought about a few names but never really settled on one. So, I came up with the one I think that she would love. "His name is Aiden Niko Phillips." She smiles at my son, then says. "Well Aiden, welcome into the world handsome." Little Aiden reaches for my finger, and I give it to him. "I am happy to see you to son." I spend a little more time letting Ayia speak to her brother.

Soon I am carrying Ayia, who is falling asleep in my arms as I head back to Karla's room. Momma Ellie is waiting for me, to give me an update on Karla's condition. "Well Derius, they said that Karla is scheduled for another blood transfusion in the morning. Robby J, and I have given blood so everything should go well. Robby J takes Ayia from me, and Momma Ellie says kindly. "Derius we are going to take Ayia home with us so that you can be here with Karla. We know that it's your face she is going to want to see first." I agree as I give them both a hug and kiss my princess good night. Franco, Shatoya, and Angela stay with me for about another hour. Franco tells Angela what happened at Friday's game. "Are you serious?! Derius it wasn't you that she saw?!"

I shake my head. "No, it wasn't me. It was this guy his name is Phillip, who I do look a lot like. He is the captain of our varsity team.

Johnisha is this stupid, spoiled bitch who thought if she did all of that I would give her stupid ass a chance." Angela sits back in her chair and shakes her head. "Derius. As soon as Karla wakes up, you have to tell her! She was so broken when she came to my house. She was crying so hard. "Why would he lie to me, Angie?" I really didn't want to believe it either, but she described you. Who knew there was another guy at your school who looks like you?! She was at my house blaming herself, because of that asshole Daryl. I screamed at her that is was not her fault and here it is it's not your fault either. I stopped talking to Dexter because of this! SHIT I have to call him now!"

Angela got up pulling her phone out and ran out of room to call Dexter. I look over at Franco who is caressing Shatoya as she yawns twice. "Franco take Shatoya home. She looks exhausted, and we know she is pregnant, it's not good for her to be up stressing about all of this either. Franco agrees as he makes Shatoya stand up and gets ready to take her home. "DK, you call me as soon as you know anything more about Karla. Do not worry about work or school I will let everyone know what is going on. You make Karla and that little man your only concern for now." I gave Franco and Shatoya both hugs as they are leaving Angela comes back in the room. "I'm going over to Dexter's to make up with him." Angela walks over to Karla hugs her, kisses her forehead, and he hugs me tightly. "You take care of my best friend; you hear me Derius?" I nod as I give her a comforting squeeze.

Angela then leaves, a nurse comes in to check Karla's vitals then she asks me if I need anything. I tell her no, and she goes. Once I am alone with Karla, I sit next to her. I admire her beautiful face, as I caress her cheek. "Beautiful, I know you are mad at me right now baby, but I swear to you, I have never cheated on you. There is not a woman in this world I want, but you." I grip her hand, holding it up to my cheek. "I promise you that ever since I laid eyes on you that you are the only woman I have ever wanted. Yeah Yeah, I know you are going to mention Keisha and Shantell. Baby that was a fantasy, they are not you. I could have had them and still would have wanted to be right here by your side."

The machine attached to Karla makes a funny sound, and I call for the nurse.

When the nurse walks into the room, I panic a little, but she walks over looks at the tubes and IV. She turns, looks at me then smiles. "She is doing fine, it's just time for us to change out her IV bag, it's empty. A sigh of relief comes over me. I lean back in the chair and watch her change out the IV bag. I have no idea how or when it happened, but I fell asleep. When I wake up, I am lying on Karla's bed. I looked up to notice that she is gone. I jump, looking around then ran out to the nurses' station. "Where is my wife?!" The nurse tries to calm me down as she explains. "Mr. Phillips, you were sound asleep, we tried three times to wake you. Your wife is okay right now, she having her blood transfusion. She has only been gone for amount thirty minutes now. She will be in there for about another three hours at the most. Please get some sleep. We all heard you confessing how much you miss her and love her. You need your strength to get through this as well. You cannot take care of her if you have not taken care of yourself first."

There is not much I can say to her, because she is entirely right. I have to get some rest. Everyone will be back here soon, and how am I supposed to keep everyone else calm with no energy. I go back to Karla's room, and with a little effort, I did go back to sleep. I tried to dream that all of this was just a bad dream and that Karla and the baby were just fine. That everything that had gone on in these months was all just my imagination. I am awakened by little hands shaking me. I open my eyes and look into my beautiful princess's eyes. I smile at her, then hug her tightly. As I sit up, I see that Karla has been brought back into the room. Before anyone can ask me anything, the doctor walks in.

"Okay well, there is good news. The blood transfusion was a great success." Sighs fill the room as we listen to the doctor. "Okay, now we have to give the treatment at least four more hours before we take Mrs. Phillips out of her coma. I want to give her some time to heal first. Being brought out of a coma can be quite scary, and we do not want her to jolt up and tear her stitches. Besides that, your wife and son are doing fine." I jump to my feet and hug Doctor Roma tightly. He gives me a big squeeze as he whispers in my ear. "You did an amazing job staying calm through this. I am happy I could give you such wonderful news." As we parted, I look at the doctor and smile. Everyone hugs Doctor Roma, then he leaves.

Everyone just stares at Karla for a moment happy that she is doing well. "I'm so happy that you made it Beautiful." We all sit around and wait for the doctor to wake Karla up from her coma. So many things run through my mind as I watch her lying there. *Beautiful, did you cry a lot when you were away from me? Did it hurt you to think I would want anyone other than you? I can't wait to answer all the questions that bother you so much. That seems to be the trigger to push you over the edge.* All these questions and more that drown my positive thoughts. "Please, Beautiful, wake up soon."

Time seems to tick by slowly as we all wait for the doctor to return. I must have dozed off a million times, but violently jerk myself awake thinking she was moving without my knowing it. Momma Ellie and everyone else went to get something to eat. They ask me did I want anything. All I could do is smile in Karla's direction as I say. "All I want is for my wife to wake up." Robby J pats me on the shoulder as he walks out with everyone to get lunch. I pull my chair up closer to Karla. As I sit there holding her hand. I can also playback everything we have been through in this short time of being married. "I have not regretted a day. I am sorry for ever making you feel I was not listening to you. I am sorry that I didn't just tell you how I felt about Daryl. I am sorry that you ever felt like I didn't love you."

I lean down, kiss her hand and lie down on it. I close my eyes a moment. I fell back to sleep and was dreaming, when I suddenly feel a hand caressing my head. My eyes open sl0wly as I lift my head, the hand slips down from my head to stroke my cheek as I stare at Karla's face. I am stunned for a moment. As I let the hand caress my cheek; I watch a smile come across her face. "If this is a dream, Lord please never wake me up." She laughs, then pinches my cheek. "Ow, Beautiful…." my words trail off as I realize I am not dreaming, Karla is awake! "Beautiful! You're awake!" I grab her, kissing her deeply. Karla pushes me back. "Hero, what happened to me? Where is the baby? I do not feel him anymore." I smile as she is still my Karla, thinking of everyone else before herself. "Beautiful, Aiden is fine. He is healthy and doing fine. How are you feeling? Is there anything I can get you?"

Karla shakes her head; suddenly she looks at me with a straight face. "Did I dream it? I smile at her; I know exactly what she is asking me. "Beautiful, you had a terrible nightmare that this man had forgotten that he promised his life to you. It's not true; I am yours forever." Karla smiles at me, as she kisses me. "So, you didn't do anything with that girl Hero?" I shake my head. "You didn't see me, Beautiful; you saw my teammate, Phillip. That girl took my jacket and watch, then had him pretend he was me without him knowing it. Shatoya found my jacket and watch on the hood of my car. I'm so sorry that you that you even went through that Beautiful. I would never cheat on you, and I will never leave you...ever." I plant a kiss on her nose. She laughs then pulls me for a deep kiss.

"I love you, Hero," I smirk at her as I stare in her eyes. "I know." Doctor Roma walks into the room. "Aw, you are awake now, good. I took Karla out of the coma, while you were sleeping Derius. I thought it would be a better surprise to have her wake up as you woke up too. I'm so happy that it all worked out." Karla smiles at the doctor. "Thank you for everything Doctor." Karla then pulls me in for another kiss. "I'm awake Hero, did you miss me?" I laughed kissing her on the nose. "You know I did, welcome back Beautiful."

CHAPTER SEVEN

MENDING MY INFRINGED HEART

At that moment, all I can do is smile at my Hero. I was so happy to hear those words. My heart could finally be at ease knowing everything I have been going through was not real. As I slept in that coma, I dreamed about my Hero and me. I had let Daryl work his evil over me for far too long. Now to hear this whole time, my Hero had someone after him also! It is just too much to deal with at one time. Before I can say anything else to my Hero. All the people who love me come inside. My mom is crying as she kisses my face and caresses it. "Momma, I am fine." She smiles at me then hits me on the arm. "OW! Momma!" My mom continues to hit me. Yelling at me about not taking care of myself.

For doubting Derius's love for me and letting another man spoil me. I look up at Derius "I'm sorry Hero, you had to worry about me." He shakes his head then kisses my nose.

Soon I see the doctor, he tells me I am doing well. He tells us I need to stay at the hospital for a few more days to recover from surgery. As soon as the doctor left. My bubbly princess was in my lap giving me hugs and kisses. She complained that I had slept too long. We all laugh, thanking God that this had not been a terrible experience for her. A few minutes later Angela walks in with Dexter. She gives me a huge hug. "I was going to kill you if anything happened to you." We both share a cry, then hug again. I sit there and listen to how everyone was doing while I was asleep. Most of it is about how Derius didn't leave my side. He missed work and school. I punch him in the arm because he should have gone to school at least. I was happy to hear that he would rather flunk than leave my side though. Soon a nurse comes in with a mobile crib and inside of it, is my newborn son. He is alert and smiling at everyone. My heart is full of happiness just looking at him.

Hero picks him up, kisses him on the forehead, then hands him over to me.

I am a complete a mess by the time I give him over to my mom. "He looks perfect." Tears slowly fall from my eyes and as my son takes my finger in his tiny hand. Hero kisses me on the forehead. "Hey little man, this beautiful woman is your mommy." His eyes seem to twinkle as he stares up at me. Hero then interrupts us as he smiles. "This is our royal son Prince Aiden Niko Phillips." I love it, it has such a great ring to it. I feed Aiden, he is such a greedy little busybody. We all take photos with our little family. Ayia really loves her little brother. The two of them kinda play with each other for like an hour. Soon it is getting late, and everyone is leaving to go home. I look at my Hero. "Hero, go to school tomorrow, it's okay. I'm fine."

Hero looks at me then shakes his head. "I will not leave my wife in the hospital by herself. What if something happens to you while I am away?" All I can do is smile and caress his face to reassure him I will be fine. "Hero, I will be fine. You need to get back to your studies and to the team. They both need you. Aiden and I are fine now." Hero looks down at his hands, then back at me. "Beautiful, are you sure? I mean I should go back now that you are awake. I just feel guilty leaving you here alone." I slap him on the shoulder. "You make it almost seem that I cannot function without you, Mr. Phillips." Derius sits next to me with a sly smile. "You can't, Beautiful." My mouth flies opens as Derius kissing me again on the nose. I push him away from me, looking at him with a frown on my face. "HERO! That is not funny." Derius grabs me, and I try to get out of his arms. "Hero, let go of me, that was just mean." Derius tightens his grip on me, kissing my forehead. "Oh, don't be that way Beautiful."

I am still trying to get out of his arms. "Let me go Derius." Hearing his name, makes Derius squeeze me tighter. "Who are you talking to Beautiful?" I can do nothing but laugh as Derius tickles me until I agree that I need his help. I keep teasing him calling him Derius until I see the smile leave his face. He lets go of me and turns his back to me. I know that he hates hearing me call him by his first name. I wrap my arms around him. Hero doesn't move to look back at me. So, I slide over closer to his side, pulling him back enough, so I reach his ear. He leans his head back on my shoulder. I smile at him, he is such a baby sometimes. I kiss his neck to his ear and then whisper, "You are not still mad at me, are you, Hero." Derius's eyes slant in my direction. I give him a sly smile and wink at him. A smirk is what he gives me as he grabs the back of my head and kisses me deeply. Our kiss sends shivers down my spine. After all this time, he still makes me feel like the sexiest woman in the world. As our kiss ends, Hero turns around and looks into my eyes. "I am not mad at you anymore. As long as you know, I am your Hero and always will be."

Tears build in my eyes as I stare at him. This is the man I love so much. Despite his age and his boyish charm never gets old. I wrap my arms around his neck pulling him down with me as I lie on the bed. He leans over when we are nose to nose. "I can never doubt you, Hero, I might doubt myself sometimes because you are so wonderful. I know I know you hate when I do, but I sometimes feel I am dreaming that I am this happy with you."

Hero kisses my forehead, then my nose, and ends at my lips. "Do you think, I don't think it's a dream sometimes? That this incredible woman, with all this talent and success, could still be in love with a mere college freshman." We both laugh, it's true our love story is one for the ages. Who would have ever guessed that I would fall in love with such a young guy?

Hero suddenly stretches then bumps me to scoot over. I scoot over and make room for him to sleep in the bed with me. "Hero you know this bed is too small for the both of us, don't you?" Hero smiles as he wraps me in his arms pulling me close to him. "Ah, I haven't had a goodnight sleep since they put you under, I will sleep like a baby tonight." I shake my head, turn to face Aiden in his crib. "Night Aiden." Hero pulls me in close to him, I snuggle back to him as he spoons me. "Night Hero." Hero kisses my forehead then snuggles up to my head. "Night Beautiful, night son." We both fall asleep, the only little person that is missing is Ayia, but she is with my mom and dad. At first, I can't sleep, I listen to Hero and Aiden sleeping soundly. "Aw my men, are so cute when they are sleeping." I feel my body being squeezed and I know that Hero has missed me. I pat his head tenderly. "I missed you too Hero."

Before I know it, I have finally fallen asleep. I am awakened in the middle of the night. Aiden is hungry again, LOL. So, I get up and feed my greedy little Prince. I burp him, and he passes back out. I look over at Derius; he is still asleep. I think of all that has happened that landed me in the hospital. I shake my head, *Nice Karla, you get sick, almost lose this beautiful little boy and your wonderful husband. Girl, you better get it together. You know for a fact that Derius loves you. He has proven it time and time again. It's you Karla that has to stop over-thinking everything. It is just not worth all the heartache and pain.* I finally yawn again and go back to sleep. Hero snuggles up again, mumbling: "Beautiful stop thinking and take yo sexy behind to bed." With those words, I smile and drift off to sleep.

I am released from the hospital about a week later. I have to take it easy because I had a C-section. So, I take a small leave of absence from work, and I get back in touch with the people who mean the most in my world, Ayia,

Aiden, and my Hero. Within my time off, my life goes back to where it was in the beginning. I am once again just a lovesick woman with my heart and mind in the clouds. Hero goes back to school and work. He is also still a dream to watch on the court. I watch him, Franco and Dexter play one day outside, while Ayia plays on the playground. Aiden is sleeping his stroller as Shatoya, Angela and I plan her baby shower. Angie admits that she is falling in love with Dexter. A few days later my sisters and brother come visit me while I am at home.

We have a family dinner, we laugh and cry about all that has happened. Before long, my leave is up, and it's time to go back to reality. I am ready now, and I know as soon I get back I have to face Daryl. The Monday I go back to work seems like a typical day. I wake up, and Hero pulls me back into bed. "You have at least two more hours before you have to go in Mrs. Phillips, how about cuddling with Mr. Phillips before you get up?" I laugh as I struggle to get out of his arms. "Maybe for you Mr. Phillips, but I have a nine o'clock appointment this morning. Angela had said one of the small businesses we loan to is about to complete a huge merger with one of our larger sister companies, and I have to be there to make sure all the documents are in order. I have to get up Hero." Derius gives me a smirk, I do not like his smirks in the morning because of what they usually mean…. Just then I can hear Aiden calling for Ayia and us too.

Derius smiles then nodded as he hops out of bed. "It's my turn Beautiful, get ready for your meeting." I smile, as I watch him go off to do his daddy duties. I am picking out my clothes when my phone rings. I pause for a moment as I look at the caller id. Urgh, it's Daryl! "Hello Mr. Dewight, what may I do for you this morning." Daryl clears his throat. "Hello Karla, I know that you are coming back to work today so I was making sure you will not be late for your meeting." I try to stay calm because this man really gets on my fucking nerves! I mean this is not my first large-scale closing merger, and hopefully, it will not be the last. He talks as if I have no clue how to handle this position.

"Daryl, do you not have any confidence in me and my abilities to do my job? I mean you have known me longer than anyone. You have my resume, and my last boss would have never recommended me for the position if he was not sure I could handle it." I listen to Daryl sighs on the phone. "Well, it's good to hear you are still yourself after the ordeal you just had. I am completely confident in your work ethic Karla. I wanted to check on you is all. See you at work." I roll my eyes as he hangs up the phone. *URGH, that fool gets on my nerves!* I thought to myself as I continue to collect my things to get dressed. Hero and I have gone through enough drama for the rest of our lives. I will let nothing else stand in our way. I shower, get dressed and head for the door when I feel myself being pulled back. I look behind me to see Hero smiling down at me. "If you think you are leaving without breakfast this morning, you have another thing comin', Mrs. Phillips."

I allow Hero to lead me back to the dining room. I smile big as see the banner on the dining room wall, it reads "HAVE A GOOD FIRST DAY BACK AT WORK MOMMY!" I look down and see briefcase shaped pancakes and car shape eggs. "HERO! This is so cute." Hero shakes his head, then points down at Ayia. "It was all her idea, I helped her out with it." Ayia beams from ear to ear "You like it, Mommy?" I laugh as I hug my Princess, my Prince, and my King. We have breakfast, and then I head off to work. Everyone greets me back to work as I enter. Angela catches me up on all I have missed. Then we prepare for the meeting. We have the meeting, and it is a great success. We all walk out for lunch. "I will have those papers faxed to as soon as possible Mr. Williamson."

I shake hands with everyone as they leave the bank. Angela pats me on the shoulder. "You did excellent my friend, I am so proud of you." I smile then punch Andrew DeMarc in the shoulder. "If it were not for this knucklehead, we wouldn't even have the merger." Andrew smiles, then bows his head as he leaves the bank. The next person my eyes make contact with is Daryl. He smiles and motions for me to walk him outside. Angela grabs my arm then whisper in my ear. "Don't back down girl." I pat my best friend on the hand as I walk out with Daryl. We are now standing in front of this car.

Before I can say anything, he starts with this: "Karla, you did an amazing job today. You really have made this place your own, I am looking forward to great work from you in the future." I smile at the compliment, but then that smile fades. Daryl knows what I have to say is not about work at all. He rubs the back of his head, then looks at me. "Daryl, I want you to listen to what I have to say, can you do that?" Daryl nods and then sighs as I continue. "Daryl Dewight, you are the most amazing person I had ever had the chance of knowing. We shared some good and bad times in the years you have been in my life. There will never be another like you, and that is why you will always have a special place in my heart." Daryl smiles, as he listens to me go on.

"However, what I need you to understand is, I am married now. Even though you may think Derius is just a child, or he doesn't care for me in the way you would. That is where you are deeply mistaken. I don't care that he is younger than me. I don't care that he doesn't have a Fortune 500 company. I don't care if he can't buy me the world. The things you can do for me physically, Derius does what I need mentally. He is always my biggest supporter. He never gives up on us, even when I let the world get to me. He loves me unconditionally. There is nothing I need that he won't try to provide for me. I never stress when I am with him. I am at peace with myself and the world when I am with my Hero. Oh, and yes Derius is my Hero. He is everything my superman should be. So, from now on, you will respect my Husband, do you understand?"

Daryl nods at me then say. "Karla, are you sure about him, for real. I mean is that who you really want?" I place my hands together, then sigh. "Daryl. I am sure about my husband. Yes, I will admit, I got swept away in the fame, the presents, and of course you. You were my first love. You never forget that person no matter if you married or not, but Derius is the love of my life. I would not change that for anything in the world. I heard how you worried about me in the hospital but not our child. Now Daryl, how selfish is that. If you truly cared about me, then my child should have been part of that concern. See, it is that selfishness that kept us apart. You act more like a child than Derius ever has in that regard. He is more mature than you, when it comes to love and matters of the heart. That's why he is my Hero. Nothing will ever change that. So, if you can't accept that I am gone and that I am married. I am fully ready to quit this position and leave here today. Daryl has a surprised look on his face. "Karla, you would give up this opportunity for him?! I mean I know this is all you have worked hard for and dreamed of ever since college!"

Everything that Daryl was saying is true. I had dreamed of being a bank manager for as long as I could remember. I love my job; I love the pay, and I love the position. It was like my ultimate fairytale come true. "Daryl, you are right I love this job, the pay, and everything, but I love my family more. I can get another job, I can get another position. I don't want to, but if I can't work with you without all the unnecessary distractions and issues…" I sigh then smile nodding. "I cannot work here any longer." Daryl looked down at the ground, for a long time. After a while, he looked at me, then smiling.

"You really would give up everything for your family. I was wrong Karla, you have not changed. You are still the same; it's me that changed. I realized what I lost way too late. I admit I let my arrogance get the best of me. I thought I could show you I could love you better than him. I see now I was wrong. Just like when you dated me and you could see only me, I see that now you can't see no one else but… "What is his name again?" My mouth flew open rolling my eyes at him as he laughs. "Derius is his name." Daryl nods still laughing at me. "Yeah, Derius. Hey, I never called him by his name before, but I will tell you something. I see he loves the hell out of you. When he punched me at the hospital and snapped at me on the phone. I'll be honest my blood boiled, but I could see it and hear it. Derius truly loves and cares for you in a way I never could."

I stood shocked at Daryl's words. Could it be Daryl Dewight was admitting to me he was wrong?! Daryl saw the look on my face and sucked his teeth. "YES! I was wrong about your boy toy!" I started to say something to him, but he had his hands in the air, laughing out loud. "Okay, Okay, your husband… Derius right? All jokes aside, Karla I do not want to lose you as an employee. My personal feelings aside. You have done amazing work here. The clients love you, your staff adores you, and Angela would kill me if I let you leave. So, it's your choice, but I would appreciate it if you would stay. I will respect your wishes and your marriage."

I am so happy that Daryl finally came around. I smile big and sigh. "Well, I am glad you see it my way because I have no idea whom you would get to replace me." Daryl nods smirking at me then leans closer then whispers "Angela." I am shocked as I hit him in the arm. "You would replace me with ANGELA?!" Daryl laughs out loud till he looks up. He nods, as Derius walks up next to me. Derius wraps his arm around my waist, and I lean against him. Daryl nods again, sighs then says: "You are a good brother, Derius, you better take damn good care of Karla, okay. Don't make me regret letting her go. You got that?" Derius nods at him then squeezes me. "I hear you, Daryl, so we are good? No more trying to kidnap my wife behind my back, huh?"

Daryl opens his car down and as he gets in says "Nah, she has finally chosen who she wants, just don't let her regret it. I gotta go."

We both watch Daryl drive off in his car. As soon as he is out of sight, I turn to Derius. "What are you doing here, don't you have school?" Derius smiles down at me. "It was an early release day. I thought I would come and kidnap my wife for lunch." I smile at him as I walk to his car. I really love his man, he never stops amazing me. I may have had a hard time understanding this love, but now I genuinely do, I would not give it up for anything in the world. Derius and I have so much to learn from each other and so much more to fall in love about. I can't wait to spend the rest of my life with him and our children.

No relationship is perfect, believe me, I know. I have had a real roller coaster of time dealing with dealing with all that has to happen with Derius. However, through the ups and downs, I am still so happy to be where I am now. As I look over at Derius driving us to lunch. I can feel the flashbacks of our entire relationship till this point. So much drama, issues, and close calls, but through it all I love how I can smile and still be right next to him. "Beautiful, are you okay?" I hear Derius ask me as he looks at me. I smile, this makes me happy. His attention to my mood and the way he always cares. I smile back at him as I hold his hand. "Yes, I am fine." I look out the window still beaming at the feeling I have. I am finally happy with my life, my family and this man I will forever call my Hero.

.

About the Author

Chimia Y. Hill-Burton was born in Chattanooga, Tennessee in December of 1981. She was raised in Giessen, Germany. Chimia is the proud daughter of Arline Agwai and Eric Hill. She is the eldest child of four children, her brothers Henry, Lemuel and sister Hadijah. Even as a child Chimia had a great imagination that she use to entertain her friends, and family. Chimia's creative talents started at twelve years old and flourished then after. During her adolescent years, Chimia continued to write, stories, poems and figurative writings were all her favorites.

Chimia graduated from John McEachern in June of 2000.

Chimia then attended Chattahoochee Technical College where she majored in Criminal Justice. After graduating in 2004, Chimia attended Mercer University receiving her bachelor's degree in Social Science in 2008. Chimia wrote the manuscript for Beautiful & Hero in 2008. Chimia currently resides in Atlanta, Georgia

"My passion for writing is a testament of the thoughts, troubles, joy and happiness of the human heart."

Sincerely

Chimia Y. Hill-Burton

Made in the USA
Columbia, SC
06 August 2020

15782967R00138